THE BRIDGE OF SAND

John James

THE BRIDGE OF SAND

Published by Sapere Books.

20 Windermere Drive, Leeds, England, LS17 7UZ,
United Kingdom

saperebooks.com

Copyright © The Estate of John James
The Estate of John James has asserted his right to be identified as the author of this work.
All rights reserved.

No part of this publication may be reproduced, stored in any retrieval system, or transmitted, in any form, or by any means, electronic, mechanical, photocopying, recording, or otherwise, without the prior written permission of the publishers.
This book is a work of fiction. Names, characters, businesses, organisations, places and events, other than those clearly in the public domain, are either the product of the author's imagination, or are used fictitiously.
Any resemblances to actual persons, living or dead, events or locales are purely coincidental.

ISBN: 978-1-80055-625-6

And what the troops shouted back at me gave me the key: 'We're off to the Bridge of Sand to find the women!' They were going where Agricola had sent us, but that was a minor detail. They were going where the moth women had told them to go, they were taking what the moth women offered, the promise of wheat and gold, wine and girls. Whatever I said, whatever even Crispinus said, they would go there.

1: THE CAMP

It was all a shambles, a disaster. That was not how the despatches went, of course. Whoever heard of a military report telling the truth? No practical man, a soldier or a merchant or a builder or a moneylender, ever tells the truth. It's bad for trade. Nobody would put any money into a business which told the truth about its dealings, which really listed the profit and the loss, which said who in management was responsible. Least of all historians who keep the public accounts of states. Only poets tell the truth. Only a poet ever knows what really happened. I was not a poet then.

It was already all over. The talking was done, the deal made. The savages' king had given up. Now the General could order the assault.

This was a High King. There were a score of little kings in the western lands, on either side of the Severn, who had made great and solemn oaths to come and fight with him, for him, when he called. Some of them were powerful indeed. By all accounts they could have brought a hundred men, perhaps two hundred, each. Most of the men would have swords, or spears, or would bring a few stones to throw. But when the High King called, the little kings did not come, because it was the harvest or the beer-making or the sheep-counting, or because they had misunderstood the message, and would come next year or regretted not having come last year, or because the messenger had found something more interesting to do on the way and had gone off to his own drinking or love-making or to settle his own quarrels. Therefore the High King, with all this support, was willing enough to exchange his High Kingdom for what he was promised. This was a house under the Palatine, and a score of slave girls with three to be changed every Saturnalia, and a bucket of gold every Ides of March, and a little place for the summer, three hundred acres or so, near Aquin where I come from.

But the General was missing something. He had never won a Mural Crown. It was the one decoration he still lacked, and coveted. Because he knew that if he wore these medals, the badge of the fighting soldier, the new drafts of recruits would look at him with respect and proper fellow feeling. The old sweats knew what they really meant, but Agricola wasn't interested in the old sweats. They were committed already. So we provided Agricola with his Mural Crown, we old sweats and the High King.

The High King and his army were encamped inside an old fort, on the top of a high round hill above the Severn. We looked up at the white stone walls. We could hear the spears rattling inside the cooking pots, and it sounded very threatening, but the General had made the deal, and we trusted him. And a High King never breaks his word.

Agricola led the way. The men would never have believed in him otherwise, or followed another officer. Attacks on these hill forts are always expensive, and it's much simpler just to sit around outside and wait till they run out of water, which doesn't take more than three days at the most. The General lumbered heavy up the hill, the leading cohort in line close behind him, but no man risking his wrath by passing him. Or risking anything else, either, by being the first to arrive alone. I tell you, a Mural Crown, a real one, is worth its reputation. Camnas had one. I wouldn't go after one for all the gold in China.

This was a safe run. Only the High King, standing on the rampart alone, let fly with a few stones at the General, carefully aimed to fall never closer than about twenty paces. He kept his bargain. The great man was the first to touch the rampart, a miserable bank of dry walling, beneath the King's feet. Then the legionaries of the front rank pulled it apart, stone by stone.

The King's men were standing inside, bewildered, with their spears and swords stuck point down in the ground, as the King had ordered. There was a confused minute or two of killing weaponless men, enough to look respectable and to give the historians something to write about. But they were only men with white hair, or one eye, or men who limped or showed half-healed wounds which were sure to swell up and turn foul in the slave barracks and kill them anyway. Most of the men, the strong ones, had to be saved for the slave-dealers, who were already on their way up the hill. After all, it's the main export of the Island.

The King came forward, in all his gaudy finery of green and white striped shirt, of copper and glass on his shield and his helmet and his armlets. There was only one good item — a collar of beaten gold on his chest. But even that was beaten as thin as glove leather and weighed nothing at all, really, when we melted it down. The High King laid his sword in his conqueror's hands. Agricola was pleased to receive it, with polished words of compliment to a gallant foe. Then the primus pilus of the Second, walking with portly dignity as became such a senior centurion, due to retire next year and go off to enjoy his pile somewhere, bound the King's wrists with symbolic chains of silver, fine as threads. The King was put into the General's litter. A double team of bearers carried him away down the slope, swearing at his weight and telling the world that it was harder to carry a man downhill than up.

I had a troop of my Illyrian cavalry in support in case we were needed, although my men said it would have been easier to carry the horses up. We only had to watch, while the General stood waiting for his litter to come back for him. The camp was spread out below us, the gaily painted tents of two legions and six wings of cavalry, one of them mine. There was Agricola's own tent, between the separate lines of the legions, a villa in leather, seventeen rooms, that took a hundred men to erect or strike. Within the fort there were one or two houses. I suppose the largest must have been the palace of the High King. They were built just like the usual houses out there in the jungle or in the swamp. They would have made a circle of posts stuck in the ground, perhaps two concentric circles for this big one. And these would support the rafters, sticking up in a blunt point. The walls would be filled in with panels of basketwork. The roof would be covered with turfs cut from the ground, and the grass still growing. To hold the walls up they pile turfs against them outside, perhaps to chest level. It didn't look like a house, but like a mound of earth.

There wasn't much in the houses: there never is. The infantrymen took all there was: a few bronze pots and the weapons — metal always comes in handy for mending things, and it's scarce out there in the bush. Then they set fire to the basketwork walls, and the houses collapsed one by one, into real mounds of earth.

The slave-dealers were marshalling the prisoners, stripping them and pushing them about, sorting them for quality. Agricola watched and took notes to make sure he wasn't being cheated. Nobody ever cheated Agricola twice. Nobody ever failed to give him full measure who didn't suffer for it after, tenfold. The dealers' men comforted the prisoners with the thought that if they were lucky the King might buy a few of them in to harness to the plough on his new farm that Caesar had given him. But they didn't believe it till men started pulling the ornaments from their heads and arms, to pile where Agricola could have the bullion valued separately. This was the first time they knew they had been betrayed, not defeated. They wept and screamed in anger, but the whips stopped that.

When the sorting was over, and the branding started, I left the Second to look after it. I took my men down the hill. We would have had the worst of it if there had been any fighting — thrown in to save the infanteers, making a charge to cover them when they ran down the hill, and then getting down ourselves.

The General tried to hold a Triumph that afternoon. Some of the Headquarters Cohort were told off to make a spontaneous demonstration of their respect and admiration for their great leader. They carried him on their shields around his tent. Then they brought out a chariot we'd captured a few weeks before, and they had some of the biggest prisoners pull it and the best-looking youngsters to walk behind it loaded with chains — iron ones. But they did not bring out the King, who was kept in the General's tent. The Second did some cheering, but the Twentieth, who'd done as much marching and not got even a cooking pot out of it, sang dirty songs at him, maliciously. My men, like most of the cavalry, didn't even bother to watch.

After that, a formal order was given for a night of rejoicing and an extra issue of wine. Not that this meant enough wine. Double the half-ration, my squadron commanders would complain, and double that again, and there still wasn't enough for a small man with an empty stomach to get halfway drunk. Perhaps a little merry, but that was hardly better than nothing. We stretched our claim a little. Tarkul, our quartermaster, inflated our ration returns with dead men and horses' godfathers, and even then there wasn't enough to be worth sharing out. We treated all our returns the same way, for fodder and weapons and food. And for remounts — if we had got half the spare horses Tarkul asked for we'd have had two mounts for every man.

But troop horses were always difficult. They had to be brought in from Gaul, because there was very little breeding of great horses in the Island, Perhaps the crossing took the stallions' minds off the job; I couldn't say the same for my men, convenient though it would have been. All you found in the jungle were those light ponies that would pull a chariot till they near strangled themselves, and charge three times in one day, but would never carry a man.

The troop commanders did the usual thing. They issued the usual half-ration all round. Then they diced for the extra issue, winning troop to drink the lot. At least about forty men would get drunk, which was something in the wineless desert, between the clay sinks of the woodland plain and the jungle-covered hills of the west. Over there it was desert — wet desert. The rain seldom stopped, and when it did it left the ground semi-liquid, too soft for horses and no use for men except to bury them in.

While the winning troop were drinking their wine, the duty troop commander, Pepan, came in from the horse lines. With him was an orderly from the Headquarters Cohort. He made the man walk through the dung piles out of a sheer sense of spite, to show what feeling a real soldier always has for Headquarters, and what a cavalryman thinks of infantry. The orderly had not enjoyed the experience, because he had been over-clean when he set out and his decurion would expect to see him even cleaner when he returned. He spoke no Illyrian, and my men refused to speak Latin to him on principle. He came to a crashing halt that rattled the tent-pole, and delivered his message which he had been made to repeat a hundred times before he set out.

'The General will see the most honourable Prefect Juvenal immediately.'

I was not going to give even a private soldier the pleasure of seeing discipline less rigid than he ought to have been used to, or of thinking I was ever not turned out well enough to see a general. So I said as languidly as I could:

'A horse!'

Vinak, my batman, spoilt the effect by scratching his behind and replying:

'I'll see if we've got one clean.'

Luckily, he had just finished grooming the troop horse I usually rode, a big ill-tempered black beast, which my men, being Illyrians, called Whitey; it had a taste for biting and a habit of leaning and a perpetual desire to go somewhere its head wasn't pointing. Vinak helped me up, and the legionary fell in at my knee as if I were under escort. He marched stiff and straight and regular, so I stifled the urge to trot and make him run. Instead I took advantage of his virtues, and kept time. I let Whitey lean against him. The bored horse managed to step on his foot twice. The second time we were passing the horse lines of the Fourth Numidians, Scipio's Own, and in hopping away from the horse he fell into a dung heap. The troopers first laughed and then helped him out by pushing him back in. When we reached the door of the General's tent, he was wet through and filthy dirty. He held my foot to dismount. I tossed him the reins and said:

'Hold my horse. Let no one else touch him. I repose all my trust in you.'

I left him standing stiff as a post, adding to his natural discipline and stupidity a sheer screaming terror of Whitey's teeth. And I can't say that I blamed him — I never got on that beast without someone to hold the head straight.

I took the sentries' salute and commended myself to Janus on the threshold, crossing it right foot first, because there was no point in facing Agricola with the slightest duty left undone. I went through the tented atrium, awash with seven days of rain not drained away. For a man born in Gaul I thought the General's devotion to ancient custom a little extreme. And I didn't like his taste in furniture, either, far too heavy for a moving establishment. But at least it looked as if it had cost a lot.

Agricola, our great and gallant General, the conqueror of the Island (with any luck) was having dinner at his own table. Nobody else was. There were four other prefects of horse and half a dozen tribunes of infantry. One of them was Crispinus of the Twentieth, a languid youth with more luck in gambling than even a rich man deserves. I guessed we poor horsemen were supposed to be overawed by the socially superior company. They were standing at attention and looking very hungry, and thirsty. Agricola was drinking wine. He had a girl cuddled up against him, a young Brit with yellow hair. She looked frightened, as if she'd known of his reputation, which would have been impossible as she wouldn't have known any Latin. But it wouldn't have taken much worldly wisdom to see that such a ravaged face and flabby body couldn't have belonged to an innocent boy. He was gnawing a ham bone, and at his leisure he asked me:

'What's your strength? Your establishment's five hundred. How many have you really got?'

'I have a hundred and sixty-nine men mounted and fit to ride,' I told him. 'I have twelve men without horses.'

'You seem the strongest. I'll send you.'

'To Gaul, General?' I asked hopefully, but he ignored me.

'You others, let him have his twelve horses. Three each.'

I saw a chance of making something on the deal, whatever it was. I objected:

'At that rate I'm still short of thirty-six remounts and twenty-two packhorses.'

'You can take packhorses from the main train. Take over another dozen horses from, each of these … gentlemen.'

'I'll send mine over tonight,' offered Ambaal, wanting to impress Agricola with his selfless devotion. I laughed at him.

'Tarkul will be over to take his pick in daylight. If you are awake by then.'

'When you have quite finished,' said Agricola, mildly for him, 'you may go back to your duties if you can remember them. No, not you, Juvenal. You can stay.'

That was a little surprising. Now the others were gone, I was conscious of a curious rattling and scraping noise coming from one of the other rooms in the tent. There was no knowing who might be listening. I stood waiting while Agricola disposed of a mouthful of honeyed figs and washed it down. He belched, and then said lightly:

'That was one of your better efforts today, Juvenal.'

'I don't understand, sir.'

'In charcoal on the floor of the chariot so that I had to keep looking at it all through the Triumph. I've got it by heart, already:

*Once there was a thin general — that's a fable
With about as much substance as a magistrate's tax returns.
If the Age of Fables returned, we'd have to work like horses,
And geldings, not stallions — pleasure's for other people.'*

'It almost scans,' I commented. 'I wonder who thought of it?'

'You'd be a fool to admit anything,' he told me. 'That one you did on the bath-house wall in London seared men's eyeballs when they read it. There's one or two of *them* would like to be sure who it was. But I'm supposed to keep the peace. A clear reputation might do you good next year when you go home and enter politics. There's no living in being a poet.'

'I'm not quite a poet,' I objected. 'Somehow that conveys the wedding of true content with strict form, in any of a myriad well-known ways, not throwing words together like a swarm of lettered bees to sting pain to the eyes, or set the brain all whirling in a storm. Poets don't feel emotion. A mind that plays the spinning top, or blows too cold or warm wastes strength and time, fritters the verseful days. Cold observation is the poet's norm.'

'You'll need to *show* emotion when you're in politics,' Agricola warned me, 'but there's no need for you to *have* any. Now, verse-maker, what are we doing here?'

'In the Island?'

What indeed? Thirty years in the country and nothing accomplished. The great fraud for the old Emperor, the march across the friendly country sown thick with wine merchants, and after that the Army was committed. But not at peak strength. Nothing here now but legions well under establishment and third-line auxiliaries not fit to fight a real enemy. Half of the force needed for policing the frontier towns, with their traders not even as civilized as the Brits now most of them had gone native and behaved no more Roman than their nonsense names. And for the rest of the force — why, every raid into the settled parts had to be followed up by a punitive column. You couldn't call them that in the despatches, so they turned into great campaigns of conquest for the record. Every high tide of marching was marked by a fortress that couldn't be abandoned, because military honour might recover from the shame in an hour, but how do you ever tell the Senate that the Imperial Eagles have retreated?

So half of the already half-strength regiments are tied up in camps all along the roads we have to build just to keep the forts supplied. And the men and horses that are used up carrying food to them, although all on the unit rosters, are no military use to anybody. Here we were, chasing a little king who had done nothing more than make a dozen raids on small towns outside Gloucester, which only existed because the Army gave them a market. And with two legions, in theory and by number in the List, Agricola had about twenty-five hundred real soldiers on foot, and not eight hundred auxiliaries, mounted or running barefoot naked with slings, to hide them.

'We advance,' I told the General, 'the blessings of our glorious Roman Law and State. For people who don't want them.'

'Finish it off,' said Agricola. 'That's the word from Rome. Now that this man is done for, who threatened the quiet country, perhaps we can advance.'

'Not this year,' I warned him. 'The summer's over, we won't be able to move when the rain comes. And we'll have to retire at once to wherever the Army can get wheat.'

'Or have wheat brought up to us.'

'Bringing up wheat takes a lot of carriage.'

'There is wheat coming, and wine. Enough for the Army to move on.'

'Move on to where, General?'

He laughed, and poured himself more wine. He'd drunk three men's rations while I was watching.

'To where the wheat is. You've heard of Ireland?'

I had. Enough to make me not believe in it. There were tales of this island to the west of Britain. The Brits said it was where the dead went, to live again happy with the Gods. There wasn't much hard fact in that. I'd never met anybody who'd been to Ireland, rising from the grave not being a popular custom among the Brits. So nobody could tell you anything definite, like how long it took to get there beyond the time of a death-rattle. So I told Agricola straight:

'It doesn't exist.'

'This is my second tour in Britain,' he told me, still mild.

'Yes, General.' I tried to sound respectful, but we all heard at least once a week that he'd been here before and knew it all. He rolled on.

'In Aquitania — that was my last province, you know — they all say the same thing, that Ireland exists although they call it Brasil, and that it's twenty days' sailing from the coast, westwards. So they seldom go there, and never come back. But if you go down into the south-west of this Island, where I was in the spring, they'll tell you it's only two or three days' sail to the west. What do you think that means?'

'Oh, one lot or the other are lying,' I told him. Obviously he wanted me to say that so he could show me how clever he was. He told me, with a wise air:

'Men don't lie after what we did to them. What it means is that the southern coast of Ireland runs a little north of east to a little south of west. And the Island is bigger than anyone thinks. It is immense, twenty or thirty days' sail broad, or even more. And I have testimony to that, as well as reasoning it out.'

He preened himself, as if he were the greatest geographer of the age, not merely a third-rate city politician who had bribed and wormed his way back into a province where he already had a bad name, because he wanted to make the money out of it he'd been too junior to steal the first time. He went on explaining.

'I have been interrogating other men in the last few days. If you go north-west, into the hills over there, for ten or twelve days, you pass great mountains to where you can walk dryshod from Britain into the next island — into Ireland. Not over land, but over sandbanks with pools of water. And you know what the Brits get from there, from that nearest part of Ireland?'

'Gold,' I said. That was easy. Everywhere outside the Empire is practically made of gold till we get there. But it always seems to evaporate as soon as our invincible Army brings to it the blessings of civilization. Which is why the Empire must always be growing, because only virgin lands bring gold. 'And bloody big dogs,' I added, because I was tired and thirsty and didn't care any more, that day, what I said, even to Agricola.

'Now, if you wish to succeed in politics,' the General told me reprovingly, 'you must stop thinking in such simple terms, and turn your mind to useful things. Things more valuable than gold. Over that strip of sand, from the next island, the Brits in the north and west get all their wheat. They call that part of Ireland the Mother of Britain because it feeds them. Just think, Juvenal, over the narrow Bridge of Sand lie great fields of wheat all the way to the great sea that lies east of China.'

'So?'

'We have a safe way across the south of the Island now, from the ports opposite Gaul as far as here. There is no point in making our rule secure to the north and east. Our way lies north-west. That will bring us wheat for the Army here — and even for the Army in Gaul. This king, what's-his-name — Druorix, that's it — that we took today, was the High King of the north-west, and held the way to the Bridge. We must get to the Bridge quickly, before another king, perhaps an Irish king, can seize it.'

'This Army can't march,' I told him. 'Even if it were the campaigning season, even if you have wheat coming up from the coast, it takes a legion ten weeks to go a five-day march, with all its gear to carry and its making of paved roads and its building of walled castles that take three days to finish for a one night's stay. Besides, we're out of wine.'

'Oh, there's wine coming in with the wheat. Ordinary ration stuff, quite good enough for the troops. Not what you and I are used to, of course. This' — and he raised his silver cup, drained it, and kicked the girl to fill it again — 'is from Aquitania. I picked up a few vineyards there, cheap, around the middle reaches of the Garonne. You might do worse than invest there yourself. I can put you in touch with a good estate agent. There'll be wine for the troops, but not up to this standard.

'Now, what you have to do is simple. Take a small mobile force, go straight across country and establish yourself across the Bridge of Sand. On both sides. The other side, anyway. Then wait till I bring the Army round the coast. Winter or no winter, this Army will march.'

'That's all?'

'That's all. You see the point, don't you?'

'Oh yes,' I told him; I was hungry and tired. 'We get hold of this year's wheat harvest in Ireland, for the Army, before the Brits waste it or it all goes off to China.'

'This year is a minor detail,' said Agricola. 'What does Rome live on?'

'The whole world lives on wheat,' I answered, rather stupidly and trying not to sound cross.

'Rome does,' Agricola agreed. 'And the wheat Rome lives on comes from Egypt. Egypt is Caesar's own property and has nothing to do with the Senate and People. Or the Army. If the Army had its own private granary to feed itself — and Rome — as rich as Egypt and coming practically overland and not across the chancy Mediterranean — why, where would Caesar be then? *Who* would Caesar be then?'

I whistled, and not only because Agricola would want me to whistle. It was better to pretend anyway that he was possessed of superhuman intelligence and shrewdness, because that's what all generals think about themselves. What tune Caesar would whistle if he heard a whisper of this I did not care to think. On the other hand, if it came off, and I had a hand in it, it wouldn't matter what Caesar thought. I returned to reality, which was disturbing enough.

'So you want me to take my ala off into the mountains at the end of the summer without any guides?'

'Oh, you'll have guides,' Agricola assured me. He heaved himself on to his feet. He was a big man by nature, and paunchy and obese by misuse of nature's gifts. He needed to lean hard on the girl to get himself up, but once he was erect he kept a firm grip on the nape of her neck. I followed them into the next innermost chamber of the tent, designed for a serving pantry where the wine could be opened and food kept hot on a bath of boiling water. There were four men there. I saw three of them at once. One was the camp commandant, a tough, very senior centurion named Pamphilius, and with him he had two legionaries from Headquarters Cohort. The flooring planks were up, and the fourth man was almost hidden in the hole he was digging. It was a square hole, deep now but not long or wide enough to make a comfortable grave; living with Illyrians makes one a connoisseur in such matters. He was down to his own chin in the earth.

I looked down at him. The King was naked, and his shoulders were raw where they had flogged him to make him dig. He was gagged with a stick between his teeth, secured behind his head with a strip of his own green and white shirt. I raised my eyebrows at Agricola.

'There's no point in wasting good farms on savages who won't appreciate them,' he told me, quite seriously.

'You'll take it then?'

'The Emperor has already allotted it as part of the campaign expenses. It would only go to waste otherwise. Here!'

The General held out his hand, and a legionary put a javelin into it. Agricola was standing behind the King. He thrust downwards, the point going in towards the base of the ribs as the man stooped, piercing the stomach and intestines. The King slumped forward on his spade. The soft iron head of the spear bent. Agricola tried to pull it out, but it wouldn't come. He looked at me, but I stood still. It was Pamphilius, obviously used to such little emergencies, who lent a hand: he came to us from Five Alaudae, never a legion noted for clean manners. Between them they managed to tear the iron, rather messily, from the flesh. No longer held upright by the spear, the King crumpled to the bottom of the grave. Bloody foam came from his mouth, he made little moaning sounds and his limbs jerked.

One of the legionaries leant down and pulled the spade from under him. They began to shovel the earth into the hole.

'Well, that's the end of Druorix,' Agricola observed in a complacent way. 'Not too full now, leave room for her.'

The girl seemed to understand. She began to sob, quietly. Agricola took no notice and explained to me, as one old politician to another:

'We don't want any of the Brits around here to know what's happened. As far as they know, he took his pay. We get rid of him, open the way to the Bridge of Sand, discredit the local rulers, and get a reputation for being good paymasters all at once. Economical, eh?'

I did not answer. Instead, I spat into the grave. It was not politic then to make any other offering for the spirit of an enemy who had run rings around my regiment for months. The gesture was ambiguous enough; in my heart I devoted the King to Janus. Agricola roared with laughter. That was when I knew for sure that he was drunk; not harmlessly drunk beyond control, but dangerously drunk, beyond piety, destroyed. He spluttered:

'That's right, fix the dirty savage.'

He hoisted up his tunic and emptied his bladder into the hole, on to the surface of the soil which still stirred gently. I shrugged. The Gods' intentions were plain. Pamphilius joined in. I asked:

'How does this bring us to the Bridge of Sand?'

Agricola looked at me with acted cunning.

'No way at all, Juvenal. That was merely in passing. Come further.'

We went deeper into the labyrinth of leather passages. In the back part of the system was a dark place for stacking rubbish and dirty plates. Two men were sitting on the ground. They had iron collars welded round their necks, and were chained by these to a post. They had been badly handled, and not in battle. Their faces were bruised, and I recognized Pamphilius' fine Syrian hand. One of them was young, slightly built; his shirt had been flogged from his back. The other was older, grizzled. He was shaking from head to foot. He wore only a strip of dirty green and white cloth about his waist. He had been branded on the chest, burning out both nipples. Another man stood against the wall, in the shadows. There was a single lamp burning, not well trimmed.

'There are your guides,' said Agricola, in triumph. 'I had a good deal of trouble finding anyone in this batch of prisoners who would own to knowing anything about the Bridge. But we got there in the end. The King told us about these two, when he thought it might mean he could live. They wouldn't talk when we worked on them direct, but they weakened when we began to flog the King.'

'Do they speak Latin? Or Greek?' I tried not to sound sarcastic. Luckily Agricola was too drunk to take notice of such subtleties. He snapped his fingers.

'You can have one of my own interpreters.'

The man came forward. He was one of the several dim figures who formed Agricola's staff, secretaries and writers and couriers who might ride to Rome with messages too delicate to trust to the memory of a soldier. Slaves, freedmen, clients we never knew. This was one of the dimmest of them all, a man with black curly hair, but light eyes and a pale clear skin, who wore others' cast-off clothing as if on purpose, and talked to no one.

'I brought Drusus with me from Aquitania,' Agricola told me. 'You can trust him.'

What he meant by that was '*I* can trust him'. It was natural that he should send one of his own puppets to keep an eye on me.

'You speak the Brits' language?' I asked.

'Moderately well,' Drusus answered in good Latin.

'He does better,' Agricola put in. 'He speaks Irish; he has an Irish name I can't pronounce.'

'Callum,' said the man, so softly I hardly caught it. I asked:

'Are you Irish? Is Ireland really a very wide land? Does it go to the edge of China?'

'The kingdom from which my father came out stretches as far as the heart can desire, as far as the heron can fly.'

'You have travelled across it?'

'I have never been in Ireland. The wise and generous General sheltered my father when he was driven from his throne.'

Agricola ignored this conversation. He turned his back on Drusus and led the way to his dining-room. He lay down on his couch and waved the girl to pour him more wine. The jar had been refilled while we were out. I asked:

'Can those Brits ride?'

'So long as they can march as fast as infantry it will be good enough.'

'I'm not an infantry colonel,' I reminded him. 'It's above my station in life.'

Agricola laughed.

'There's infantry going. A cohort of the Twentieth.'

This was bad. I had thought for a little while that I was to have my own command, a chance to win reputation, to get something to boast about when I got back to Rome, to give me a leg up on the ladder of office. But — infantry!

'Whose cohort?'

'A mixed lot of hastati. Crispinus will bring them.'

So that was it. Here was the man of the right family, the man who could expect automatic advancement to a magistracy, not because of what he had done, or even of what his father had done, but of what his ancestors had been before Hannibal came. Commands were for men like that. But I knew better than to argue over it. I asked instead:

'What's the use of sending cavalry, General, if you're going to load us down with flat-feet? I thought you wanted us to make a quick dash across the mountains.'

'They're hastati,' he reminded me. 'They're supposed to be *light* infantry.'

'The difference being,' I said, 'that they can rise from sitting unaided, instead of hoisting each other up like the main body. They can't move any faster.'

'I want that bridgehead fortified.' Agricola was firm. 'I want to be entrenched there for the winter. I may not be able to reach it with the rest of the Army till next spring if the snow comes down too early. That's what infantry are for. But they'll never live by themselves in the mountains. The cavalry are for escorting them, and guarding them while they do the work. The Twentieth are my own regiment, remember. I don't want them thrown away.'

'So I'm tied to the apron-strings of the infantry commander? And him not walking by himself yet?'

'Don't you understand, Juvenal? It's a very pretty promotion for you. I'm giving you a mixed cohort. There's an establishment of a thousand men, and pay to match it. I must send you. I've been watching you, Juvenal, and this is how I can have someone on this column with drive and bite and a touch of savagery. Who else would I send? You wouldn't have me put Crispinus in command?'

'But — you can never put a prefect of horse in command of a tribune of infantry. It's against all precedent.'

'I'm the commander-in-chief. I make the precedents. I can trust you, Juvenal.' I remembered that he could trust Drusus, too. 'No one in the Army must guess where you have gone. I have the quartermasters stripping the Army to let you have seventeen days' rations. Wheat and wine. You can suffer Crispinus. Knock him into shape. You could have worse. I name no names.'

No, I thought, *I'll have to take Crispinus. Agricola could trust him, to watch Drusus and me. I might not be of the same exalted patrician birth as Crispinus, but at least I'd never spent the night in Agricola's tent. I'd got the post honourably.* I tried to quibble over the ration quantities — I couldn't have faced Tarkul otherwise.

'Only seventeen days? Will you be up to us by then?'

'I don't know. You may have to forage when you reach the Bridge. But hold on till we come. I don't expect to see you in this camp after noon tomorrow, or any of your smelly horses. Crispinus knows he's going with you, but he doesn't know where. The secret is yours — and Drusus's.'

He turned over on his couch, his back to me. I was dismissed. I saluted and went out. In the dusk, the legionary was still holding Whitey's bridle. He didn't see me coming, because he was looking up at a flight of cranes overhead. The horse had eaten most of his helmet plume, but otherwise he was even cleaner and shinier than when he had come to fetch me. A dozen of his comrades had been at work on him with brush and polishing rag while he stood holding the horse. Even his tunic was clean and pressed, under his cuirass. I decided not to ask how he had that done while holding the bridle. I might have to hear how many men had been bitten.

'That's what I like to see,' I told him. 'Devotion to duty. It's good enough for a light infantryman. If you keep on like this, we may let you transfer to the cavalry as a noncombatant groom.' I stopped with my hand on Whitey's neck — he needed some soothing after all those clanking infantry scuttling around. 'D'you hear that?'

'Hear what, sir?'

'Where do you come from?'

'Alexandria, sir.'

'Townsman?'

'Yes, sir.' And he sounded proud of it: no rustic he.

'Have you ever heard a wren sing in the dusk? And in the middle of thousands of men?'

'Birds is birds, sir, and does what they like. All except the ibis, praised be his flight.'

I gave him up and rode away. I tried to think about wrens, those harmless little birds. Anything was better to think about than Agricola. My last sight of him was bad. He had forgotten me before I reached the door. He was playing with the girl. He had one hand between her legs, and with the other he was grinding her face into his crotch. It was better outside. The worst to face was the smell of horse dung. It was especially strong on my senior squadron commander, Camnas, who was waiting for me at my tent door. As he helped me down, Tarkul came up.

'What am I to do with thirty-one hundred rations? I've just signed for them.'

'We march tomorrow at the fourth hour.'

'As late as that? And carrying the stuff?'

'Make us up to establishment with troop horses and packhorses from the other regiments in the morning. The camp commandant is making out the vouchers.'

'We're going a long way?' asked Camnas. I was about to think up a fitting answer when there came a wailing and shrieking from the compound where the morning's prisoners were penned, a noise of men mad with grief. It died away into a low keening.

'Some people,' Tarkul observed, 'take a long time to wake up to reality. Now, Velthre?' For that occasional use of the Illyrian address to the well-born was the only mark of respect he, or indeed the common troopers, ever gave me in private. In action, we were all fellow troopers, and we set our standards of comradeship by that. 'Did you eat well at the General's?'

'Eat well, my horse's backside.'

'We have a little put by for you.'

I followed him into my tent.

'I see you've laid out my own dishes for four.'

'We thought you might like company.'

'You fancy you can stand the squalor?'

Tarkul was the dandy of the regiment. Epicure, wine-taster, dandy — he was dressed now like a king, with a silk scarf to stop his mail collar from chafing his neck, and a tunic of pure linen. He had three gold rings on each hand. He hoarded every unconsidered obol from every shady deal, and put the money where people could see it. Vinak poured water for me to wash.

'On ration porridge we feast?' I asked.

'Wait and see,' said Camnas. The other squadron commander, Tarchies, reclined with us. Vinak brought on the food.

'Where d'you get a pig?' I was suspicious.

'Somebody out of Pepan's troop went a-foraging, about ten miles. I think it was Pepan himself, he was stood down today. We didn't see him at all. Have a drink.'

'And this isn't ration red.'

'It was that squint-eyed Cupesar in Camnas's troop,' Tarkul explained. 'I didn't ask him details, but I think that a tribune of the Twentieth had a private store, and he thought if we were moving we needn't waste it.'

'How did you know we were on the march?' I asked.

'Oh, it's been in the air all day, even before I got the ration dockets. I have my spies in the camp commandant's office. And friends too — Pamphilius may not be an ideal drinking companion, but he has his uses.'

I considered that. Then I asked:

'Where are we going? Is that in the air, too?'

Tarchies was a quiet man. He rarely spoke, and never smiled, because he had lost his front teeth some years ago and did not want to look or sound ridiculous, which indeed he often did. But since we were in private, he lisped:

'I think, if I can have a guess, that we're going over the Bridge of Sand into Ireland.'

I looked so surprised that the other three burst out laughing. I reminded myself that they had been comrades in the regiment for twenty years, while I had been in it in command for nine months. Camnas explained, leaning his thick clumsy body back on his couch.

'When Paulinus had this Army, he was always going to make a run for the Bridge. He'd sent off one small force just before we had that trouble in the East — a mixed cohort that was, too, horse and foot. Of course, once that nasty work started, we forgot all about them, and they never turned up again. Somewhere out in the jungle, that's where they are still. Paulinus thought that if he could hold that Bridge, he'd finish off those Druids. They keep on coming and going, and inflame those Brits to an insane desire for wine and good wool cloth, and the need to take them off honest traders without paying except in iron. If it weren't for the Druids, the whole lot would settle down and we could all live peaceful ever after.'

'Do you think —' I began to ask, but Camnas just talked me down, as he often did when he was imitating the sing-song accent and the wordy style of the native pedlars.

'The only question that I've been asking about Agricola, that good and wise General ever-victorious, was whether he would wait till the next dry season and move the whole Army up there, or whether he would seize this fag end of the summer and send up some gallant band of horsemen, as it might be us.'

'I can see it all,' Tarkul carried on. 'He's done this job early enough to think of starting the next before the winter. We make a dash up there, mark out the road, put the fear of death into whatever little king is trying to hold the Bridge now that the High King is gone, and come back fast into winter quarters. Then next spring we make the triumphal march.'

'It's not going to be like that,' I told them. 'We're not going alone. We shall have company. Infantry company. Don't look so depressed. There won't be many, but they can pay for slowing us down. They can do the picket duty around the horse lines and carry forage in and dung out. We won't have to lay out our own camp. No digging for us. When we reach the Bridge they can build us some winter quarters, and there we can stay till spring. We have to cover the crossing — from the other side.'

'And if all Ireland comes against us?' Camnas asked.

'Let the infantry stand the siege, and we'll ride for help,' Tarkul suggested. Into the laughter Vinak broke, standing stiff as a sentry and using his 'best' voice.

'The Most Noble Tribune Crispinus to see the Most Noble Prefect of Horse.'

We all four laughed more, partly at Vinak, partly at Crispinus's solemn face of ceremony. The wine had been good and we had drunk a lot of it fast. I decided that I would refuse to be formal.

'Come in, Crispinus. Lie down and have a drink.'

He came in languidly, selected the end of a couch with care, strung his bean-pole body where he thought there wouldn't be any horse sweat. He sipped his wine, and his face changed, as if for a moment he'd forgotten the part he thought he ought to play. I wondered if he'd ask to see the seal on the jar, but Vinak kept the napkin tightly round it. Crispinus looked around him, cleared his throat, didn't say anything. I waited a moment, then told him:

'You can say anything you like in front of my officers, Crispinus.'

'This is a little difficult—'

'Oh, they all speak Latin perfectly.'

He gulped, was unable to avoid opening, said:

'The General seems to have been rather disturbed this evening. Of course, after such an exciting and successful day, and the Triumph, it's only to be expected that—'

'He'd drink himself stupid, you want to say?' I asked him brutally. There's nothing like straight talk to put devious men off their stride.

'Oh, no, I wouldn't ever suggest that the General might be the worse for drink. But you will admit that he was not himself this evening.'

I'd never seen Agricola more himself than when he was slavering over that girl and pouring down the wine. I offered a minor concession.

'Occupied might have been a better word.'

'Well, yes, perhaps occupied. Now, in a state like that, of course, he often gets things a little mixed.'

'I've not seen him as unbuttoned as you have.'

Camnas needn't have laughed at that, it gave a bad impression.

'Well, he obviously got things a trifle confused. He was talking at times as if he expected you to be the commander on this expedition over the hills.'

'Well?' I could see my officers' expressions out of the corner of my eye. It had taken them aback — it must have hit Crispinus hard.

'But surely — a cavalry officer — it's not at all likely that Agricola would have put you in command and then sent an infantry tribune under you.'

'And why not?' Crispinus had started this, and I must have it out with him now.

'It's obvious. The Army is infantry. The Army is the legions. That is why legionary officers are always…' He decided he'd said enough, but I wouldn't let him get away with it. If he'd started to be insulting, he'd have to finish. I asked him, angrily:

'You want to say that only aristocrats can be legionary tribunes? Only nobles? Does mere birth give them the sole right to command?'

'Everybody knows that … well-born … that only…'

He was in difficulties now, he hadn't expected me to do anything but accept his cool assumption that there had been a mistake. I went at him.

'Well, what's wrong with me? Am I not your legal equal? Isn't my father a knight? I'm a better soldier than you are, that's the difference. That's why Agricola has given me the command.'

He turned on me, then shrank from my face as I showed my fury. I pressed home my advantage as he remained silent.

'I now appoint my subordinate commanders. If I fall, Crispinus, you may take command. But till then you will be the commander of the infantry. You will be of equal authority with Camnas, who will command the cavalry.' That meant a promotion for Camnas, and I wondered if I could force it through the secretariat in the morning. And a worse blow for Crispinus to be on an equality with a professional soldier, and not even a citizen born nor one who had bought the toga, but a man who had been made a citizen when he was given his rank as a reward for brute strength and courage. 'And as a new squadron commander,' I went on, to put Crispinus's appointment into its proper minor place, 'who shall we have from the troop commanders?'

'Pepan,' said Camnas and Tarkul together. Tarchies shook his head a little, then grudgingly:

'The boy may as well have his chance.'

'Right. Now for the order of march.' I had seized on Crispinus. He had come to me with this preposterous idea of taking the command out of my hands, was it not fair now for me to give him his orders? But before I could start listing the troop commanders, and setting out the order of battle, Vinak put his head into the tent.

'Velthre!' he called me in Illyrian. 'There is something out here you ought to know about.'

I went out to him. The other officers had no choice but to follow, Crispinus with them. I looked around me in the dark, and then asked angrily:

'What is it? I can't hear anything strange, except perhaps that cursed wren still ticking away, lost here in this camp and trying to escape.'

'That's just it, Velthre. If you can hear the wren, how silent it must be.'

He was right. There were nearly three thousand men around us, and nobody was saying anything. Even the prisoners in their pen were silent. Then, as so often, we heard it, well away from the camp. It was the steady beating of spears on cooking pots' a throbbing rather than a rattling. We had this almost every night. It didn't mean an attack: the Brits never liked to fight at night. But it wasn't very pleasant to hear, because you knew they were there, somewhere in the dark.

The trumpeter at Headquarters began to sound the First Alert: a steady call on the bass horn while you could count five, then a space, and the other trumpeters took it up at the third repeat. That meant nothing, only (according to the drill-book) double sentries, stood-down half of the duty cohort to stand-to, stand-by cohort to muster, duty cavalry squadron to saddle up and wait dismounted. Nothing to concern us tonight. According to the roster, we needn't move till the Third Alert, the long calls on the bass horn with five quick toots on the treble in the intervals. The noise drowned out the wren: or it flew away.

And then the noise of the cooking pots stopped. It didn't die away, it just stopped suddenly, all around the camp as if someone had given an order. I peered into the dark, and then felt rather than saw a shadow at my shoulder. Not one of my officers — they all were in front of me. Not Crispinus — he had gone back to his cohort. The shape spoke in a sibilant, nasal voice, a Brit accent but different, the Latin not perfect, the usages of Southern Gaul.

'Remember this tomorrow, when we march.'

'What does this mean, Drusus?'

'Something for you to sing, poet. Are you indeed a poet?'

'I write verses.'

> '*A poet's business is deaths and swift departings,*
> *And sudden knowings.*
> *Births, marriages and travels, deep forgettings*
> *Comings and goings.*'

'Which then is this?'

'Watch close and see.'

'After today's fiasco,' said Tarkul from in front, 'we can expect anything. Look!'

Up on the hilltop, where the High King had handed over his sword, and his men, and although he did not know it then his life, there was first a glow and then a great burst of flame. A fire blazed into the heavens. Not a little heap of sticks under a cooking pot, but a hundred trees and oil by the barrel, tar enough for a dozen ships and the fat of herds of pigs. There had not been a burnable shred inside that camp when the legionaries had finished with it — military scavengers, we always called the Second: they'd pulled the posts out of the huts to save cutting their own wood for their cooking fires. But now a furnace glowed there, enough to roast a score of oxen if we'd had them.

'It was like that,' Tarkul whispered out of the dark, 'years ago when I was a trooper. That was when Boadicea died. We were out on the north flank, but when the news came the Brits lit fires. Not one only, but many all over the Island.'

'Aye, like that,' breathed Camnas. I looked behind me, where he tugged at the hem of my cloak. To the west, where we'd be going in the morning, there was a rim of hills beyond the Severn. I knew where they were, even in the dark. On one of the peaks, or at least at the right level for it, I saw a spark of light that grew, sparkled like a star, attained a recognizable shape, turned from mere light to redness. I thought of the heaving shape beneath the General's tent, and I shuddered. There was another point to the left, growing, and then another, till all round us, perhaps ten miles away or less, was a great circle of fires. No one in the Army here knew what had happened in the wine pantry, except those who, like me, would be ashamed to speak of it. Yet the fires of mourning were lit all around us.

And is this all? I thought. We have been in the Island now for, oh, thirty years or more. We have marched about it here and there. We have built roads, thin ribbons through the jungle, and never dare to step off them. We have planned cities, and sometimes we have even begun to build them. Yet what are we still but a few thousand frightened men, huddled behind our walls, afraid of the jungle, afraid of the sheer magic of the Island? All over Britain, just now, soldiers are waking in their little square hidey-holes of earth and logs, to look at the fires on the hills and to listen to the music of spears on cooking pots, and wonder, what now? Boadicea nearly had us all. Will it happen again? Never mind about the blessings of civilization, and Imperial glory — what worries us is whether our heads will be on our shoulders in the morning. Are we going to come through the next seventeen days alive?

Only Agricola sleeps happy above the King, clutching his violated girl. He is dreaming of bribing the people with wheat, giving Rome as much as Caesar can bring from Egypt. If he can bribe the people, need he bother about buying the Senate? With wheat and a victorious Army, let who will be Caesar — Agricoia will be Imperator.

I felt that I was in deep waters. It was none of my business. It was not what a Roman thought of — a soldier obeys his orders and stands firm. When in doubt, it is always a good maxim to cease to be an individual. Surrender yourself to the drill-book. I told my officers:

'We march at the fourth hour. Either go to sleep, or start working. For myself, I sleep.'

But I could not sleep, Crispinus haunted me, his unspoken jibes rankled. I could not turn them aside, only answer them, in clumsy verses.

> *I'm a Roman, a citizen, like you and the rest. What does it matter,*
> *That my father's father was bought and sold, used to show*
> *Whip scars on his back, chain furrows on wrist and ankle.*
> *And his wife, if you can call her that,*
> *Some kind of Scythian, bought cheap to breed from,*
> *Wouldn't learn Latin. As children we were told*
> *Never to mention this. But he talked to us,*
> *Was evasive about how he got his freedom,*
> *But hinted at how he got his money, buying and selling*
> *Pigs, pictures, women, horses, land. A lot of money,*
> *And my father made more, bought up half the town*
> *Bought himself a title and a gold ring,*
> *Bought me this commission, like your father did for you.*
> *And after that, just the way you will,*
> *I'll buy a nice safe billet, collecting the taxes*
> *From a good fat town, no worry about what I take,*
> *As long as Caesar gets what he asks for. The Law*
> *And the legions protect me. For a low assessment, men pay*
> *Land, horses, women, pictures, pigs. In Rome we're all equal,*
> *All well-born — as long as we've got the money.*

2: THE JUNGLE

Of course, we didn't march at the fourth hour. Only that fool Crispinus thought we could, and he nearly went demented running round yelling at his centurions who had everything under control and who took no more notice of him than if he had been a fluttering bird. I didn't make any fuss, I just lay on my couch and watched without interfering while Vinak took my tent down from over my head and packed it on three horses. As it was, we were lucky to get out of the gate by noon, and I put that down entirely to my own placid nature.

I got a troop of horse out ahead, with their mail shirts and their helmets on, ready for action. The rest of the cavalry rode in drill order, like the infantry. I had a few men out on either flank, but the rest of my troopers rode at the rear to make sure the infantry didn't straggle. That amused them — they were good hands with whips. We put the packhorses in groups between the infantry sections: that way I saved the Illyrians the strain of looking after them as well.

I rode either at the tail of the van squadron or at the head of the infantry, however you liked to put it. Perhaps leading the infantry, since Crispinus rode beside me. He and his centurions had lost their horses months ago, and had been marching like their men, in mud and misery. I put a horse aside for the tribune out of the remounts we got from the Numidians, and I promised the centurions mounts when they had eaten some packhorse loads. There had nearly been bloodshed over making up our horse numbers, but Tarkul had taken more care than had the Numidian quartermaster to be a friend to

Pamphilius through the campaign, so we did even better than Agricola had promised.

In the very front of the column, Pepan rode with the guides on leads like dogs, sniffing out the path. Drusus rode with him, on his own horse. They didn't talk very much to him — they didn't talk to each other either, but there, I don't suppose their position was one to encourage the art of conversation. They just slouched along beside the horse.

That first day, they hadn't much guiding to do. We picked up the line of an old road that one of Paulinus's units had made years before. Perhaps that dismal crowd that had gone off to seek the Bridge of Sand and not been heard from since. Camnas had been at pains during the morning to find out all the grimmer stories he could about our destination, so as to cheer Crispinus up. Illyrians think this dark talk is very funny.

We forded the Severn, and nobody actually got drowned, which was a remarkable thing considering we had infantry who fall down easily and don't float at all. We were the first troops across the river for years. The men were light-armed, according to the book. They wore boiled leather cuirasses with only a little bronze or iron about the shoulders, and some plating on the front of their leather kilts where it helped to preserve their martial capabilities. But each man had an iron helmet, and that's the end which goes down when you fall into water. Besides, every man had his share of the section's tent and tools and one man in each section carried a handmill which wasn't a thing to forget. Apart from that each man only had an entrenching tool and earth basket, the big red cloak that was also a blanket, spare sandals and leather for patching, water-bottles, and three days' rations in a sealed pack, not to be opened except in emergency and in the presence of an officer. And they all had a jumble of things they had picked up or bought or just plain looted all over the Island, stupid things like bronze wine jugs or women's skirts. You never know what will take a soldier's fancy. The usual thing was to wrap all this in the tent leather and sling it over your shoulder on a stout wood stake. The stake was part of the tent.

The country was not definitely friendly, but at least probably safe. The men tied up their helmets and their javelins, and some even their swords, in their bundles. They slung their shields on their backs. The fourteen days' marching rations of wheat and wine were on the packhorses. The cavalry carried most of their own gear and their helmets tied somewhere on their horses, and our tents were on our own packhorses.

We forded the Severn where it was spread wide and nowhere up to a man's waist. Halfway across, I called up our standard bearer. He was a lean man with a scarred face, called Pulena, thought to be mad by those who didn't have much to do with him and known to be stark staring crazy by us who were forced to meet him every day. We were rather proud of our regimental standard. Old Manilius, who'd raised us for the Philippi campaign, picked up some bronzes cheap in Attica. So above the cross-piece which carried the banner he mounted a rather delicate bronze crane in flight, the crest extended. But the banner itself was quite conventional, red with gold fringing and a black Imperial Eagle worked on it.

I sent Pulena ahead to get to the other bank first. The legionary standard bearer couldn't keep up, of course. He did his best, passing Pepan, and I thought he'd burst a blood vessel with the effort. He was Trebius, a man well known in the Army for a wine nose, a beer belly, and four armbands and a collar for bravery — a polite term for brutal savagery in the assault. The infantry, being a cohort of the Twentieth, had a bronze boar as a battalion standard — the regimental Eagle was safe at the depot. I made up the set with my personal standard, which I'd had made up for me in Londonium. To show my origin in Aquin, I had two bulls' heads, back-to-back Janus fashion, mounted on a steel-shod staff. Vinak carried it behind me.

Pulena made the other side without any trouble. If the Gods had made his horse stumble, guided him to a pothole in the river or made a stone slide under his hoof or drifted a log against his fetlock, I'd simply have turned the whole regiment round and waited till next day. But nothing unlucky happened. Quite the contrary.

There had been plenty of the common marsh birds around, duck and coot and mallard. As Pulena came on to firm ground, there was a clatter of wings, and over us went a great flight of herons, or cranes, near enough to our own standard anyway. The horsemen shouted and cheered, thinking that some God lived in the spot and had blessed us. The infantry weren't so pleased, not smelling any roast pork.

I called to everyone within earshot:

'Follow the cranes! The cranes will lead us to our goal!'

Even Crispinus looked pleased. Only Drusus looked back, gravely, and said for me to hear:

'All men follow the heron at the end.'

He said no more, and we were too busy from then on finding the old road and following it. The jungle closed in around us, and I was forced to call in the flankers, because they could not force their way through the thickets and I was afraid they might stray too far off the road. But the narrow way was well beaten down, so that the centuries were able to march in compact blocks, two abreast.

Just about the right time, less than an hour before sunset, we came to the old camp our predecessors had built. Even after fifteen years the banks were firm and strong, six feet high. I resolved that we weren't going to waste our time or energy building anything like that for our one-night stops. The camp was big enough for two cohorts of infantry at full strength, if such a thing was ever seen in Britain. The four streets were still plain, and it was no trouble at all for me to ride to the place where the Chapel of the Standards ought to be and strike the staff of my bulls into the earth, before Pepan or anyone else came through the gate.

I went back to watch the troops filing through. I hadn't seen them pass when we left, because I was leading them, and I had been very busy since. But now I saw what I ought to have known about earlier. I called Crispinus and asked him:

'Tell me the truth. How many?'

Crispinus was only a youngster, sent to learn politics and crafty moves in the Army before he went into politics at home — just like me, except that he would get some sinecure on the strength of his family name, while I'd have to sweat gold in bribes for every place I'd hold. He couldn't have been much use with his own legion, or Agricola wouldn't have sent him out with me. Give the General his due, he knew how to train officers. Maybe he couldn't use them in any rational way, but he wasn't as witless as people made out. He'd taught me how to *use* cavalry, in less than six months, just as Camnas and Tarkul had taught me how to be a cavalryman. He had given me a man to train myself. Now I would have to ask myself what I was doing and make everything plain before I moved. Having the load of Crispinus on me would make me stop to think. So I started by making Crispinus think. He scratched his head, wondered where to look, was about to call his centurions to share the blame, but finally owned up:

'Two hundred and thirty men.'

I swore hard by every God I could think of.

'Agricola promised me a cohort.'

'We're all under strength, you know that.'

'But not that much under strength. And he said he'd make a cohort up — it ought to mean nearer six hundred than two.'

'Call it a weak cohort or a strong maniple, take your choice. Anyway, you've got four nominal centuries, with their centurions.'

That was something. No matter how many men you've got, or how good they are or how willing to march, or even fight if they have to, you can't handle them without decent officers who've been taught their job. With a few blows of a vine-wood staff, they'll make even unwilling men march and fight. These centurions looked passable, not the best I'd known, but good enough to work with.

We grazed the horses outside while there was still light, and then brought them inside the fort. There was room enough. The stream a little way off was why our predecessors had camped there. Being inside a ready-made fortress this first night gave my officers a chance to work out how to dispose the men and horses, I left them to it. After the meal I went round on a formal inspection, so that all the infantrymen could see what my face looked like and hear what the sharp edge of my tongue sounded like. I had the sentries posted according to the drill-book, marching their beats and giving the challenge every hour as if they were at the depot. The cavalrymen were very amused at seeing the legionaries doing all the work. But all the men had been at least two years in the Island, except for Crispinus and myself. They didn't object to being sentries — nobody wanted to be cut up in his sleep.

The second day was not like that. It was bad. It was very bad. It was the first of many bad days. I had expected it. The Brits themselves are our implacable enemies, and every ninth Brit is a magician, a Druid as they call them. These men can change their shapes or fly or melt into mist as they wish. And the trees are their familiars.

We had been moving along the old road through the edge of the jungle where it was not much more than dense scrub — thick to push through, but not high: you could see a long way over it from the back of a horse. The edge of the deep jungle was like a wall; trees a hundred feet high reached out their limbs to us. It waited like a swamp to suck us in.

I expected the guides to take us along the old road, but after an hour or so they pulled at their leashes like dogs and turned off towards a narrow path which cut into the deep forest like the valleys deep in the cliffs between Paestum and Surrentum. Pepan hauled back on the leads and strangled them to a halt. I came up and told Drusus to ask why they were making into the forest. After listening for a time to the question and answer which I could not understand, I began to question the usual tale you hear that Gauls and Brits and Irish all speak the same language. After Pepan had flicked them strategically with his whip, Drusus claimed he had got some sense out of them.

'They say that the road leads back to the Severn and across it to the east. This path meets the Severn a lot further west, and then we only have to follow it to the Bridge of Sand.'

I pondered this. We had already made an error in letting the two guides run together. There was no knowing how they had conspired. I decided I would have them separated. In case of doubt we could try one after the other, gagged, to see how they agreed. But now, I didn't trust them. We couldn't enter the jungle if we wanted to come out alive. I was about to give the order to follow the road, when the men began to shout:

'The cranes! The cranes!'

And sure enough, there they were, overhead, flying with lazy wingbeats. They came directly over us, over the cleft in the forest, and flew on west, always west. They were soon out of sight over the treetops, but they had made the will of the Gods plain enough. We were to follow them now as at the crossing of the Severn. I called for a wineskin and a cup, and a handful of wheat. I made the offering at the gateway of the forest, to the God that only Romans know, Janus of the Gates and Ways. And then I waved my little army into the forest where no Roman had been before.

At first I was able to keep the men going in a double file — even the cavalry, although they bumped and bored each other. But soon the path was too narrow for this and we found ourselves strung out in a long single file, every man keeping far enough behind the man in front to avoid being speared on his carrying pole or kicked by his horse. I would have liked to have flankers out, or even to have got all the cavalry off this one path, but it just wasn't possible. I moved some pioneers forward, even in front of Pepan and the guides, to cut the worst growth away, but this slowed us down badly. The day before we had come ten miles in three hours; today we would be lucky to do ten miles altogether.

Soon it was plain that the pioneers were not enough. We all had to fight against the jungle because it attacked us. The trees did not want us to pass. The branches struck out at us, tearing at our eyes, knocking off our helmets. The roots, as we watched, twisted themselves out of the earth to trip us. The thorns grasped our clothes, making jagged holes, for all the world as if they were teeth to gnaw at linen and wool and flesh. There was a malice here that we could feel and see. One bramble bush pursued me, leaping out at me from one side, clawing at my face and arms, and then running on ahead to take me on the other flank when I least expected it.

Things happened to delay us. A man would be brought down by the grasp of a root: he would fall all ways along the path, scattering his belongings. Sometimes he would break his carrying pole; it would take time to redistribute his belongings over his own harness and among his comrades. Then a packhorse tripped and broke a leg. We had to kill it, and pull it off the path — it happened, of course, where the undergrowth was thickest so it was hard to get rid of. We had to get the corn sacks off it and give a sack extra to the nearest other horses, which refused to start while they were overloaded, knowing to an ounce the weight allowed them by Imperial regulations.

We kept on. The day before had been sunny, the sky only half clouded. This morning there had been a complete tent of grey cloud over us, and as the morning went on it hung lower and lower. I didn't like it. About the fifth hour it began to rain, as I had feared.

We have no rain in Italy like they have in Britain. There is not merely a lot of rain, there are a hundred different kinds of rain, and, Drusus told me, each has its own word in a language which has no single word for rain as such. And each kind is unpleasant. This was not a heavy pelting rain, where the distinct drops bounce from a pavement: this was a thin drizzling penetrating rain that soaked through armour and tunics and flesh, drenching us to the bone. I halted the column so that the men could put their cloaks on, and this was a wrong move. It wasted time, and it made sure that all the cloaks got wet. The infantry only had their issue cloaks, all alike and all red and all just about thick enough to hold water. Perhaps they had been good garments when the commissariat bought them in Fabius Maximus Cunctator's day, but they had been issued and re-issued and slept in till there was nothing at all left of the substance but the dye. The cavalry had all been able to buy, or acquire somehow, their own cloaks. We all went in for the native manufacture, made in the Island out of good imported Roman wool. They'd only just begun to bring real Roman sheep in to the chalk lands along the sea. These cloaks were properly made to suit the climate, very heavy and close woven and retaining the natural oil to keep out the water. No two men had quite the same cut, or anything like the same colour — you never can get two alike. But I did insist that our cloaks should each be of the same colour all through. No stripes for us — that's what the Brits wear. My own was a dense weave in russet, the nearest I could get in that quality to the deep red the officers wear in the legions. I pulled the cowl over my head and tried to pretend that it wasn't happening. I had been in rain before, but never in anything of this quality.

The rain kept on all day. At about the ninth hour we began to wonder if we would ever find a place to camp. The forest was thick around us. The men were getting very tired. Their leather shields and cuirasses soaked up the water and weighed them down. When we had only two hours of daylight left, I heard a trumpet from in front of us. I pushed my horse forward along the path, shoving the men aside, and came up with Pepan in a kind of clearing. Along one edge of it ran a stream. Here we could camp. I dismounted, walked forward and thrust my standard into the ground. The surveyors came forward with their measuring sticks, but there was hardly room for them to work. We called the cavalry forward, and sent a patrol out of the clearing on the other side. Then I had Crispinus bring the infantry in with axes, and when they had dropped their packs we in our turn could attack the forest. We cut down the trees on the edge of the clearing, and as each fell we stripped the branches from it. The trunks were moved forward, following the retreating forest edge, till we had enough space to get all the men inside and the horses too. We had to cut down more trees to make an open space around our camp before we could fence it with logs.

The legionaries are good at this kind of work. My men, of course, had enough to do with their horses, pegging out the lines, cutting grass and carrying water. But the rain kept on and everything was wet. It took nearly an hour before we could start a fire, so that when the rampart was completed the men still had no hot porridge. Vinak brought me my own wine and cold ham while I superintended all this work of fortification.

When the men had finished their building and seeing to the horses, they put up their tents. The leather sheets were wet through and took twice as many men to handle. But I saved time by walking around as I ate and encouraging them to greater efforts. This seemed to have some effect on them, judging by the increased animation of their looks and gestures. I insisted on a thorough inspection when the camp erection was finished, and found fault with the grooming of both men and horses. This ensured that when the men were at last released they were able to go at once to their food and did not have empty time waiting in which to grumble.

The two guides we shackled by a ring-bolt to a tree-stump. When all was done, and the sentries posted, I could go to my own bed and listen to the rain on the tent roof.

I slept well, tired out by the day. But I woke, as always, a little before dawn came. Almost as soon as I moved on my bed, Vinak brought me a cup of wine mingled with warm water, and Army bread, wheatcake, not leavened with yeast. He brought my tunic, warmed, and my cuirass, and held my toga while I put it on. I waited till I was sure that the sun had risen, somewhere beyond the thick cloud, and went to the Chapel of the Standards. By the presence of the boar, the cranes and the bulls this booth of wood and leather became a temple sacred to Janus. I had not thought it worth putting up separate chapels for the infantry and cavalry, so I spared my Illyrians the burden of erecting their own tent. But I had brought out my own bronze tripod, as more fitting than the plain Army issue, and my own incense. The incense you get from the quartermaster is cheap government issue; if the Gods, especially the Emperor, are worth worshipping at all, it's only prudent to do it in style.

Pulena had got the charcoal glowing. The signarius sounded the Still and everyone came to attention as I said the proper prayers and sprinkled the incense. The morning before had been the first time I had done this as a commander. I had felt nervous then, but now I moved as if I had done this every morning since I came into the Army.

The men were already waiting to take down the Chapel. Vinak took my toga in exchange for a cloak dried over the fire. I put on my helmet to keep the rain off my face. The men were taking too long to strike camp and pack their tents and gear. And I didn't like the way we had been marching. Anything could have happened to us yesterday, straggling along through the jungle all unprepared. I called the officers and told them so. From now on we would march in battle order. Every man would wear his helmet and cuirass, and the cavalry would put on their mail shirts. The infantry must carry their shields on their backs, and their javelins loose, not rolled up in the tent panels. They would have to make everything else into neat bundles on the tent stakes, so that if anything happened they could just drop their kit and be ready to fight. Of course, the men never like this, being lazy by nature. Least of all the cavalry, who have to make everything up into two saddle-bags — repacking takes them time, and thought, which is worse.

The men had to wait while the parade was completed, for sections took different times to get their things together and to slight the wooden rampart they had built the night before. So the men who had worked the hardest and best when we had made camp the night before were the last into the line of march when we left and Trebius laid into them with his staff for it. But at last all was arranged peaceably and we were able to get on to the road.

It was worse than the day before. The rain was as heavy, but this time the men were wet to start with, and would have been uncomfortable even if it had been a dry day. The path was a green way through the woods, with the branches lying back a little where, long ago, someone had tried to cut a road. But after the first horses had been over the ground it was cut up badly. The last sections of infantry were up to their knees in mud. They straggled and fell behind. We halted every three thousand paces for rest, as the regulations stated. This was barely long enough for the last men to catch up, and they had to march all day without a stop. Even so, we went slowly and what we would have done if we had waited for the men to eat before we marched I don't know. Not started till dark, probably.

It was nearly nightfall before we found a place wide enough for us to get off the road and make camp. Now everything was so wet that the men weren't able to light cooking fires. They made themselves a thin gruel with ground wheat and water. It was not much to nourish a man, but it was a little better than nothing. Luckily I had a spare cloak in my pack and I was able to sleep dry myself. Next morning I wore it on the road.

But on the third evening in the rain I had no dry cloaks left. So to show that I was not unconcerned with the sufferings of my men I had Vinak rummage in my stores and find a jar of the most precious liquid known in the Island — olive oil. Men scraped under the leaves till they found dried sticks from last year's falling, and Crispinus gave an old shirt. We soaked this in oil, and after some trouble we were able to light a fire. Vinak made a frame to hang my cloak on to dry, and then I let the men take brands for their own use. The men were now thoroughly out of sorts, their hands were bleached white and chapped by the water and their knees were as bad. Some of my troopers were wearing breeches like the natives, but I frowned on this as a general rule, since it was hardly dignified for a Roman.

The log ramparts this night were little more than a token. A line of cut sticks and blazed trunks marked out the boundaries of our camp. If we were attacked we had nothing to hold. Our shields would be our only defence. The cavalry would never get away. But I felt sure there would be no attack that night. There was not a sound in the wet forest, not even a rattling cooking pot a mile away. I heard a few birds, a late wren, an owl. Everything else was silent: no men moved beyond the ramparts.

And yet we were watched. I felt all the time that there were a thousand eyes on us. Someone beyond the rampart heard everything we said, saw all we did, knew the intentions of our hearts. Were there eyes in the leaves, ears in the stones of the ground? It was absurd, but nothing was absurd in the Island, nothing was impossible. Nothing was rational except the things we brought, the standards, the incense and the tripod, the names of Jupiter and Janus.

I walked about the streets of the camp, past the lines of picketed horses, past the sweating men hammering pegs and posts, stretching guy ropes, heaving the sheets of leather that would cover their heads. And then, in a space below the western boundary, I came on Drusus, the Irishman.

He had no leather tent. He rode one horse, and carried his bag and his food on another. He did not wear a sword, but he had a sickle and a billhook. He had cut and worried at the brushwood and built himself a booth of boughs and leaves faster than any of our men could pitch a tent. He had closed the doorway with a branch of rowan, the berries beginning to turn. Now he stood outside it, his hands outspread. I waited till he finished his prayer, and asked:

'What offerings do you make?'

'What need of offerings here?'

Perhaps his Gods did not need offerings. The Gods below take nothing except for the obol beneath the tongue; they take not ours but us.

'I worship,' Drusus told me, 'the Gods that are.'

'The Gods of the Island?'

'I worship the Gods that are, in the Island as I cannot in Gaul, in the woods as I cannot in the pastures and the grain fields.'

'Who do you worship? What are their names?'

'We call them Taran and Esus and Teutates —'

'That is Jupiter and Mercury,' I translated, 'and perhaps Mars.'

'No, these are the Gods that are. The Gods of Rome have no place outside Rome, beyond your camp. But here we know Lug of the Silver Hand, and Arianrhod the Castle Maker, and the Lady of the Birds and Flowers.'

'Do the Gods of the Island bring the weather?' I asked. He might know what offerings would bring dry weather.

'They are the Gods,' and he dismissed me, without further word spoken, without flicker of expression, without change of tone. I was sent away. And I went away.

In my own tent I ate my supper of toasted ham and wheat cakes and drank wine. I heard the rain beat on the leather above me. It was dark. Crispinus came to me, moving quietly through the camp in his sodden cloak. He entered as Vinak announced him, giving me no chance to deny him. I poured him wine, and he spilled a small libation before he spoke — to Chance, I suppose.

'Tomorrow we turn back.'

It was not a question, it was a statement. I looked at him angrily.

'Who has made the decision?'

'The decision is made for us, Juvenal. We must turn back. Winter has come too early. This is not campaigning weather.'

'That has nothing to do with it.'

'It was wrong to let a cavalryman command a mixed force. Can't you see the state the men are in? They're not horses.'

'I have orders to march, and none to turn back.'

'I have given the orders to turn back. I have warned the officers that tomorrow we return.'

I tried to keep calm. Raising my eyebrows when I would rather have raised my hand, I asked:

'You have told my officers?'

'I have told my officers — and yours.'

I did not answer that they were all my officers, and he was too. It would have left him chance for a sterile game of contradictions. Instead:

'You think they will obey?'

'They obey the logic of necessity.'

'And you will face Agricola?'

'He will understand. I'll lead the next expedition to the Bridge. But in the dry season.'

'Your head will fall when I tell him.'

'Not my head, but yours.'

He was probably right. I had not had the pleasure of the General's attentions through a season's evenings in the camp. Crispinus probably had the advantage of me. But there was no doubt that logically he was right. That Island is about the size of Italy, but nine-tenths of it is covered with the dense, humid, chilly jungle. It was madness to expect men to fight in it in the wet season. But I was in a cleft stick. I could not go on and live. I could not return and survive.

Before morning I had somehow to think how to outwit Crispinus, how to make the decision to turn back my initiative, not his. Had he been talking to Camnas? He would have used his enormous prestige as a patrician, junior tribune, potential ruler over thousands of citizens born, while Camnas was a citizen only by favour and bribery — how else do you get Imperial favour but by bribery? If he had been at Camnas, then Camnas would desert me. Camnas must resent that I should come out from Italy with no experience but a minor tax-collector's job in Campania and six months as junior tribune in a legionary headquarters in Spain, and take an ala when he would have given his ears for the chance. I did not answer.

It was then the thunder started. I stood up, and took my cloak. I told Crispinus:

'In a thunderstorm we have to look to the horses.'

The troop commanders were quite capable of doing all that themselves, but I wanted to show Crispinus that there was more to do in the cavalry than sitting waiting for orders. I went out into the rain.

I moved to the forward edge of the camp, by the fence I had had them build along what I hoped was the north side, to the gate through which I intended we would march in the morning. There was a sentry there, of course. I walked up close to him, as if we could shelter each other from the storm. I asked him, after the absurd formality of challenge and countersign:

'What is your name?'

'They call me Achilles.' He was a big man, thick of arm and leg and belly, with a hoarse voice. 'That's because I have so many weak points.'

'Have you seen anything? Or heard anyone moving?'

'Not much to hear, most noble Juvenal, only the owl and the wren. And now this thunder.'

'The wren? But that's not possible at night.'

'Oh, in this horrid country, sir, anything's possible. Owls by day, bats that sleep head up, anything.'

'So you've seen nobody?'

'No, sir, only the Goddess.'

'What do you mean? What Goddess?'

'We've seen her a couple of nights, sir, us on sentry go.'

'You haven't told any of the officers?'

'Well, it's none of our business, unless we're asked special. She's out there tonight. You watch the next flash, over there, down the path.'

'How do you know she's a Goddess?'

'Well, sir, she's … well, she looks like a Goddess.'

'Which Goddess?' I was asking, when the lightning came again. And some way from us, down the path there was someone, a pale shape, standing, watching us. It was dark again, at once, and my eyes could not see, dazzled by a brightness greater than the lightning. When I was able to look again I could make out the pale shape, still there. I asked Achilles:

'Have you seen her close?'

'All dressed in gold and silver she is, in robes of silk of Samos, mystic, wonderful. Her face is fairer than the rising sun, that men will only look on after prayer, of hues —'

'Have you seen,' I cut him short, 'the statue of our Lady Venus of the Sea at Lutetia?'

'Oh, yes, most noble Juvenal, I saw it when we marched up here first.'

'And you have the story off very pat, that the priest tells.' I closed my eyes against the lightning again. When the last roar of thunder died away, I said:

'I will go out to her.'

Trebius had come up to us, softly. He objected.

'It is too dangerous. I'll send a patrol of legionaries out there instead. This man can go first, he seems to know all about it.'

'No, I will go.' I must show the legionaries that I was one of them, that they were mine. 'Give me an infantry shield and a short sword.'

'Take mine, sir,' Achilles offered. I told him:

'You'll need them. You're coming out with me.'

A little crowd of off-duty soldiers had collected. They shifted the tree trunk we had put across the gap in the fence to stop the hobbled horses straying. I held the shield in front of me, I kept the sword hidden under my cloak. And we went forward.

The pale shape was a hundred paces from the fence, no more. The mud and the wetness of the grass squelched round our feet. But the way was clear, no roots tripped us, no brambles tore at our clothes, no branches struck us in the face with human strength. Yet I looked down where I stepped, I did not lift my eyes to see what, who I was approaching. I waited till I could smell the horse she sat on. Then I looked at her, over the rim of my shield.

It was indeed the Goddess, seated there. Her horse was white as a lily, she rode cloaked in gold upon a golden saddle cloth. Her head was crowned with an arc of gold arching like a peacock's tail from side to side. The rain poured on us, but her garments were not dampened. Achilles stood behind me, and we looked on her in silence till I knew she willed me to speak.

'Gold I give you, Lady, that bar my way.'

I spoke in Latin, but somehow I knew the form of words proper to whoever this was. I fumbled at my throat and unpinned the brooch that fastened my cloak, a poor thing but still a pin of gold, set with a small emerald, pear-shaped. I held it up, and then threw it on the ground at her horse's feet. I snapped my fingers at Achilles.

'Have you any gold, man? Give her *something*.'

To my surprise he took a gold coin from his wallet, a small one but still shining pure enough in the next lightning flash. He said something under his breath, grudging, and tossed it far away from him. The Lady bowed her head. The sacrifices were accepted.

'Now let us pass, to ride to the Bridge of Sand.'

And she replied. I did not know the language, but I knew the meaning and the strange form of her words. Her voice was like the pipes men play for sweetness, not like any voice I had heard before. I knew her meaning, as if she had said:

'Out of Aquin the Ox shall come,
To Britain the home of the Constant One,
To bring to Ireland the rule of Rome,
And lay her dues in the Bridge Maker's Dome.'

I waited. My thought was confused, my heart paralysed, I could not understand what she meant, except that it was an answer to me, was for me. I cried again:

'Lady, let us pass, to make the Bridge!'

She only answered:

> *'Go back, King Roman, and hide in your walls*
> *From the mists that rise, from the rain that falls,*
> *From the trees that strike, from the stones that fly,*
> *Hide, Roman, from all under our Island sky.'*

'Do you forbid me?' I asked.

> *'Go back, Roman, to your bitter town,*
> *Where nothing matters but the Emperor's frown;*
> *The Fates will lead your footsteps up, not down.'*

'I will not be forbidden,' I said, quietly. 'I am a Roman, and where I have said I will go, there I will go.'

I looked her full in the face, and her grey eyes cut to my heart. I had known women before, but never a face like this, never a meaning in eyes like these that burned into me. I knew that it was my fate to follow where these eyes led, whether forbidden or let. And above all — I stepped towards her in the rain and the rumbling of the thunder. The thorns snatched at me, the branches struck to force me back. I dropped my unpinned cloak to free my arms, and I cut about me with my sword. I told her:

'This is Roman iron, that doesn't bend when I strike. I am as strong as the iron, and not to be turned away. Whether you bid me or ban me, I will come to you, across the Bridge of Sand.'

I stepped towards in despite of her own words, and she punished me. I saw her bend, I heard the singing of all the Gods, and I felt her reach out in a glory of light and take the sword from my grasp. And then I slept, peacefully.

3: THE VALLEY

I woke in my own tent, on my own bed. It was greying into day, but the dawn was only new. I could hear the first birds, the lark, the thrush, and, above all, the wren, many wrens. I pushed aside the cloak and stood in my loincloth. Vinak was at my side, with wheatcake and wine, and warmed water to wash my head and hands. I put on my tunic and my toga. There were soldiers about the Chapel. They looked at me strangely. I offered my incense, and the trumpeter blew the Stand Easy. Now Vinak asked:

'Most noble Juvenal, are you well?'

It was a strange question. I could remember all that had happened in the night, except one thing. I asked:

'How did I get into my own bed?'

'After … the God visited you… Achilles brought you back. He carried you in.'

Camnas came to see me, in the light rain.

'The lightning struck you,' he told me. 'We all saw it. Your sword melted with the visitation of the God.'

'The Goddess,' I corrected him, but he did not seem to hear. He went on:

'The men will be ready to march as soon as the Chapel has been struck. Crispinus had them paraded an hour before dawn. He says we are to return.'

'Are we?' I asked him, trying not to challenge.

'The men will not go on. We must go back. The forest has been too much for them. The horses are in a very bad way as well. We've got a dozen men too ill to march, but they'll cling to their saddles somehow till we get back. The infantry — we'll have to load about thirty of them on the packhorses. We're in no condition to fight, even if we could march.'

'When the men are ready,' I told him, 'sound the Assembly.'

I went into the centre of the camp. The guides were still shackled to their posts, eating some scraps of food Vinak had thrown down for them. There was a tree-stump here, a wide one, cut off about two feet from the ground. That would do. I stood on it while the men fell in in front of me. To my right, the legionaries in their sodden red cloaks, their painted shields; all the same yellow. On my left, the cavalry in their motley mixture of cloaks, every shield painted different so we could recognize each other in action. The officers stood in front of me, facing their men. I could not see Crispinus's face; I returned his salute without peering too closely beneath his helmet brim, drawn down against the rain. I looked down on my little array, and began:

'We have been days on the forest road, my brothers. We have come by a hard trail, cutting our way. We have had the rain in our faces, the wind tearing our shields from our arms, pushing us off the path. The trees have fought against us. It would be a reasonable thing to turn back.'

I paused, and for a moment nobody took advantage of it. Then it was Crispinus, who led off with, 'Yes, we'll have to go back.'

A lot of the soldiers joined in the shout to go back. It sounded pretty unanimous, but from my stump I could see that most of the men, and all the other officers, remained silent; waiting, I thought, to see which way the cat would jump. I waited till there was silence, till well after the silence had come again. I began to bless my father for insisting that I went to elocution lessons. I'd learnt to use silence as a weapon. I waited till the shouting had died away, and the longest shouters were feeling sheepish. Then I rubbed it in.

'So? We are beaten. We were sent, all of us, each of you as well as myself, to defeat the forest. We were told to cross it. Remember, no one fights for what he does not want to defend. The forest and the weather have fought against us because the men of this place do not want us to pass. Shall we go back and tell Agricola that they beat us in three days without a fight? What will Twenty Valeria Victrix tell Two Augusta? What will the Illyrians tell Scipio's Own?' I waited for this to sink in. *Now*, I thought, *I'll show Crispinus who knows how to train soldiers.* I whirled on the legionaries, and yelled at the top of my voice:

'Who are we?'

And they came back immediately, as one:

> *'We are the Twentieth from Rome,*
> *Hard as iron, tough as stone!'*

And I turned quick to the cavalry, and shouted at them too, like the drill sergeant does at the depot:

'Who are we?'

And they replied at once, repeating without thinking the old cadence:

> *'We are the Cranes who kill in the light!*
> *We are the Cranes who ride by night!*
> *Don't come out if you don't want to fight*
> *The Cranes!'*

And both units cheered, and Trebius raised his standard high in the air. Pulena leaned down and crossed staves with his own banner.

'So! Are we beaten?'

'No!' the men all shouted back at me. The officers still weren't moving, and I wished I could see Crispinus's face.

'Which way do we march?'

'That way!' the soldiers shouted, pointing out of the gate, the way I had gone the night before to meet the Goddess. And as if in answer, as if she or Another had sent it, there came immediately on us a great storm of hail. The slingshots of the Gods rattled on our helmets, bounced off our shields, almost cut our faces. The horses jumped and bucked, but the men were already loading the packs. The wind came harsh from the west. The pellets of ice, hard as iron, were hurled at us horizontally like a volley of arrows. It threw the men about, picked them off their feet, tore the tent packs from their hands. I laughed. And I shouted above the gale, and Janus made me heard:

'That's how much they want to stop us. Will they succeed?'

'*No!*' the men shouted, and stood to their ranks as if there were no need of sergeants. Only Achilles came to me as I got down from the stump. I expected to hear him demand something, ask for a gold coin to replace the one he had offered, or at least for a new sword for his comrade. But instead he gestured at Crispinus and asked out of the corner of his mouth:

'Shall we do him for you? We can get him in the turnings of the path out there, and nobody will ever know.'

It was a touching offer, and I was sorry that I had to decline it. But I had him help me up on to Whitey, and then rode over to where the guides were chained to their stump.

'Whose turn is it?' I asked Drusus. He gestured to the younger man. I reached down for the chain and hooked it round the horn of my saddle. 'I'll lead,' I told the troopers.

They fell back, looking at me with strange eyes, saying nothing. Only, when I reached the gate, I heard Camnas say to the leading troop:

'Make way for Juvenal, the heaven-blest.'

It was the lightning, they would follow me now, touched by the God. I sat straight in my saddle against the driving hail. The guide whimpered as the sharp pellets cut into his skin. I pointed to the north, the way the path went, and pulled at the chain. He didn't want to go. He sat down on the grass. Pepan let go at him with a long whip, but he wouldn't move, not till Drusus had spoken to him, not sharply as with an order, but gently, coaxingly.

I led the march into the wood, along the path I had followed the night before. A hundred paces? Or less? Was this where the Goddess had spoken? I drew in the reins and called Drusus to squeeze forward beside me. In front of me, the path was blocked from side to side by a spider's web, spun from tree to tree. It was the height and width of a man; the gossamer was spangled with raindrops, but not torn by the wind or the hail. Drusus shook his head, and the guide pulled back on his chain. I laughed at them.

'Who dares not, gains nothing.' I trotted Whitey forward to burst through the web. Its threads clung to my face but I brushed them away. If it were Ariadne herself who had spun it, my way was open now.

And I was right. In another thousand paces the hail changed to rain, not piercing needles of water but a soft downpour, almost a falling mist. I shouted back to the column that we were breaking the weather. The men cheered. The cloud was higher. It had hung for days on the treetops. Now we could see beyond it; we were in a valley between high hills, narrow here but opening out beyond us. We thrust forward, The wood was not as dense on either side of us, the thorns were no longer reaching out to tear us. I waved Pulena to come forward and take the guide. He rode before me with his banner scarlet and black, surmounted by the crane. We were bringing Rome into the jungle, and the jungle was not going to stop us. I called Drusus to ride with me.

'What was the meaning of what I was told last night?'

I waited for him to ask what I had been told, but instead he asked:

'Was it not the old prophecy, about the Bridge Builder and the Constant One?'

'Is it an old tale?'

'There are many forms, all difficult to understand. In some the words themselves are too old to have any meaning. But it is well known.'

'Known to Agricola?'

'He is a constant man.'

Constant, I wanted to comment, in greed and in gluttony, in lust and avarice and evil intent. I did not think it very prudent to talk like that to Agricola's client. I asked instead:

'Who is the Bridge Builder?'

'The Greatest Bridge Builder? Surely that is a priest somewhere down in Rome?'

I knew that too. And who it was. Little known now, it was the one title that Caesar must keep, the key to the worship of the City, the right to make the secret sacrifice to Jupiter and the Gods who stand shadowy behind him, and are not named. Yet... Drusus forestalled me.

'There is only one man from Aquin in this Army, who comes as a bull.'

'That, too, Agricola knew?

'When you first went to Seven Gemina in Spain, he wouldn't rest till he found a post for you. Have you ever heard of anyone so young and inexperienced being given a command like this?'

I didn't discuss it more. It was clear why I was sent. And a suspicion crossed my mind. Who was really in command? Had Crispinus a secret commission? Was this something that Drusus and Camnas knew? When the real point of choice came would they follow me? Or him? I looked around. The wood was very thin now, little more than scrub. Camnas was well trained, he had thrown out a screen of flankers without asking. Was it my orders he was anticipating, or Crispinus's he had obeyed? I wondered if I had done right to refuse Achilles' offer.

But then there was something better than the thinning wood. Ahead I could see blue sky. The rain had almost stopped. I looked back to the infantry, now marching in column of threes, much easier to handle and defend. I called to them that Jupiter was smiling on us. They cheered, and for the first time since they left the Severn, I heard them begin to sing the old song from Marius's day:

> *'You don't get much for two obols a day —*
> *There go the Cimbri over the hill.*
> *You can't keep a girl on a soldier's pay;*
> *She wants gold, or else she won't play,*
> *Once take your eyes off her and she's away —*
> *Sulla saw us and he's running still.'*

There were thirty-seven verses listing most, but not all, of the enemies of the state since then, and it took us downhill, through the scrub. The rain stopped completely. We were walking dry at last. There were one or two sickly blue breaks in the cloud. And then the clouds parted, and we could see the sun for the first time. We were not marching north, but west, even a little south of west. I kicked my heels into Whitey's side to catch up with Pepan and the guide. As I reached them we came fully clear of the edge of the wood, a hard border. We were looking across a wide open valley, a great grassy meadow, good grazing for the horses, and a stream running across the north edge of it, under the steep hillside. And the stream was running west, the way we were going.

I snatched my own bull standard from Vinak's hand, and nearly overbalanced in doing so. I was afraid that I might fall off, and bring bad luck to what I knew that only I as the leader could do. I trotted Whitey across the grass, trusting him not to stumble. When I was well clear of the wood, out in the middle of the meadow, I stopped Whitey at random. I walked forward with my eyes closed, praying to Janus to hold me up and at the seventh pace I stabbed the steel-tipped staff into the earth. It went well in, and when I stood back it stayed upright. All was well. I looked back to where the column was halted on the edge of the meadow. Nobody was risking following me till they knew the omens were right. My wave to the troops brought them marching out, three centuries abreast, the cavalry out on either side, the host of packhorses following in front of an infantry rearguard.

The surveyors reached me first. They took their position from the standard, their direction from the sun, and laid out their diagonals for a camp to hold us all. The centuries marched up, and I called to Tarkul to issue a day's wine ration to each man. They needed it. They were wet through, shivering, they were dragged down by the weight of the water they were carrying. The wine would put some heart into them. I turned to Crispinus.

'We'll camp here for a day or two.'

'The men need it,' he told me. 'It was madness to come so far.'

'Who cares about your men?' I flung at him. 'I'm thinking about my horses.'

They were in a worse condition than the soldiers. They had scarcely been groomed since we started; their coats were heavy with mud. Many were limping, and would hardly bear the weight of their riders. However, only one troop halted, for their riders to lay out the horse lines within the boundaries the surveyors had marked with stakes. The other horsemen rode through, and spread themselves out on the edges of the wood, guarding us from a sudden rush from cover. When I looked back to our way out of the wood, I saw that Pepan and a trooper were having difficulty, literally dragging the two guides out into the open. Drusus rode by, aloof. I caught at Achilles as he went past, with that air of being committed to some errand of supreme confidentiality which is the hallmark of the old soldier who knows how to avoid work.

'What do you do when we make camp?'

'I work for the surveyors, most noble Juvenal. I clear ground for them.'

'Before you start, drive in a stake for these two worthies in the usual place. Left of the Chapel.'

The sections had already laid down their packs in straight lines ready for tent-pitching. Tarkul had taken half a section to unload some wineskins, and had the first men queuing up for their extra ration. I joined the line, ostentatiously taking my turn. I could have done with the drink, but I never got it. One of the surveyors came to me at the run.

'I think, sir, you ought to see what Achilles has found.'

I went with him. Achilles hadn't driven in the stake yet. He had begun to cut away the grass with a sickle, for the Chapel, so that he could see next where to plant the stake. Where he would have driven it in he found an obstruction. It was a huge stone, three paces either way, the height of a man's chest, lying there isolated in the meadow.

'All right,' I told them. 'Put the stake in on the far side.'

'There's more,' the surveyors told me. They led me to the stone. At the foot of it, on the east side where we were, I saw a litter of abandoned things. There were scraps of bone, mostly. I found bones of deer and pig, and of the small black cattle the Brits keep up here: no bones of the big wild bulls of the woods. There were bones of birds, of goose and partridge, and little frail bones that looked like frogs. There were bones of fish, and shells of mussels and oysters. There were the shells of all manner of birds, the shards of broken pots and a few weather-rotted rags.

I looked to the top of the stone. The flat surface was pitted with round depressions, the size of a cup, where the rock had been ground out. These were stained darker, where something had been spilled on to them, and on to the stone around. For the rest, the stone was a light grey, speckled with white and with glints of mica in it. Granite in hills where there was no granite — it must have been brought there. And not by human strength, in that land where the horses were small and where there were no roads.

This was a place of offering, a table of the Gods. I was not surprised when Achilles, now clearing on the west side, called out:

'Look here, sir. Is it good or bad?'

I went round to him, stepping over his neat piles of cut grass. He had found a skull, leaning against the west side of the stone, looking out to Ireland from eyes that were no longer there. It was old and dried, fleshless, green with mildew, some teeth remaining.

'This is an abode of the Powers,' I said to Crispinus and to Drusus. The latter veiled his face with his cloak, and spoke no more — it was obvious he wasn't going to be much use. I ordered Achilles:

'Go on, clear it all the way round.'

He worked now in short light strokes, using the extreme tip of the blade. He lifted the cut stalks aside with his fingers. Then he grunted. I came to see. This was not a skull, but a head. It rested on the ground, looking towards the north, towards the Bridge. The neck was set in the open ends of a gold collar, a flat plate of gold hammered into the shape of a half-moon, thick enough to be rigid, chased and engraved with patterns of lines and whorls, the heads of beasts, of lions and wolves and bears and horses. It was the kind of collar they said kings wore in the Island before we came. And a king wore it. I knew that face. The mouth was twisted in pain and despair and hatred. The soil was still in the hair and the dried-up week-dead eyes. It was red soil from under Agricola's tent, from a hole dug again even while Agricola slept.

'What ought I to do with it?' Achilles asked. It was a tidy mass of gold; it would have meant a fair addition to the Regimental Burial Fund. But I was cautious. I told him:

'It was offered to the God. Let it lie. Drusus! What God is worshipped here?'

He spoke from behind his cloak.

'I do not know. The name is not revealed.'

I looked to the guides. They were crouching on the ground, shivering with fear, whimpering almost. I had seen men like this before, and there was nothing to be got from them. I could take no chances. I called for my toga. I offered what we had. The trumpeter sounded the Still, and all came to attention. The men digging out the ditch and throwing up the rampart inside it, the men hammering in the stakes on the bank, axemen on the forest edge cutting firewood, troopers laying out the horse lines, or carrying water from the stream — all stopped their work and turned towards me.

'Unknown Gods,' I prayed, 'who are worshipped here, accept our offerings and guard us.'

There was no need to say more. I poured our sacrifice into the cups on the stone, wine and oil and ground wheat.

'We will give more, when we have it.'

We waited for a sign, while a man might have counted seven. And then it came. Out of nothing, a haze of moths settled about the wine, as dense as smoke. And a bird perched on the stone, that we had not seen flying. It pecked greedily at the wheat, and we all heard it:

'Tick-tick, tick-tick.'

There was a noise over us. We looked up to see a great concourse of herons, whirling and circling, before they scattered in all directions, over the woods.

'The cranes, the cranes!' shouted my troopers. I turned to the soldiers gathered round.

'See! The Gods have blessed us. They have accepted our gifts. What more have we to fear?'

The trumpeter sounded the Carry-on. Achilles bent again to his work, only muttering under his breath:

'Cranes, that's all. No trouble for you horsemen, but what about us?'

He was soon answered. There was a burst of shouting from the edge of the wood. A boar came out of the brush, half a dozen horsemen after it.

The open space between the camp and the edge of the wood was full of men, cutting grass, digging, picking up wood. The boar went through them like a rock from a catapult. They scattered, shouting. They tried cuts at the boar with sickles and axes, and one man who had a javelin handy tried a cast, nearly skewering a sergeant of horse who up to then had done him no harm. (He made up for it later.) The whole clearing seemed full of men, trying to get out of each other's way and dropping bundles of grass and timbers and buckets till it looked like Ostia market place on a quarter day; at the same time it seemed absolutely empty, leaving me as the only possible target for the boar's charge. That's how a civilized place always feels when there's a wild beast on the loose.

And this time I did seem the target. The boar came straight towards the gate opening, where the bank was already waist high with stakes set in it on either side. I had seen this before, too, because the animal's natural bent when hunted is to find a thicket to lie up in, to receive visitors. And what was our camp but a thicket for the boar men of the Twentieth to lie up in? Inside the gate he came face to face with Pepan, who was still mounted with a lance in his hand.

He rode at the boar and struck down with the point the way the drill sergeants teach, but not very accurately. The beast checked in his stride, and then came on more slowly, bleeding among the trodden grass. It came to a halt not two yards from me, glared round, and then slowly toppled over. Pepan dismounted and was about to cut its throat, but I stopped him. He and I and Crispinus snatched at the legs, and as the wicked brute struggled in death the tusks grazed my arm. But we got it, somehow, up on to the stone while the blood was still coming from the wound in little pumping spurts. I cut at the neck with my sword, and the remaining blood gushed out. We had been in time. It was a living sacrifice.

Camnas came, in his toga. But he was more than a mere citizen of Rome, or an Illyrian noble. He had passed through the stages of the Mystery.

'To the unknown God,' I offered the boar. The wren, somewhere in the grass, ticked approvingly. Then Camnas took his own knife, a strange-shaped blade for such a task, and ripped up the belly at one stroke, deep down yet doing no damage. He plunged his arms into the reeking body, brought out the liver. He bent over it, turning it this way and that, mumbling old forgotten rhymes, words not heard in Italy since Tarquin's time. The trumpeter had not sounded again, but everyone was still, waiting to hear the haruspices from the Twentieth's own boar.

At last, Camnas spoke in Latin the formal words we were all waiting for, that we all understood.

'They are good.'

The legionaries cheered, feeling that their prayers were answered. The work began again. I called Pulena, who was standing guard on the three standards, plunged into the soft soil till the tent would be erected over them.

'Haven't we got our own Chapel with us?'

'That can stay packed,' he answered. 'You said we could use the footsloggers'.'

'Unpack it. Put it up over the stone. We may as well show some manners. The God may be angry if he is left in the open while our standards are sheltered.'

This was common sense. Men come to grief through ignoring such precautions. I returned to Camnas.

'Were the auguries really good?'

'They were!'

I mistrusted his short verdict.

'We are not lost, then? We will triumph?'

'Lost? Triumph? Those are other matters.' When the God was on him, when he acted as a priest, Camnas thought in other terms from ordinary men. 'In a week we will find what we seek.'

'In seven days then? Will we find the Bridge of Sand and conquer, in seven days?'

'In nine days,' he corrected me. I ought to have known that he would use the long week of the men of old. 'In nine days each of us will find what he seeks. No more can I say, and no less.'

I gave up. After a while he would return to sanity, but there was no sense in him while he was being religious. We left the liver and the heart on the altar, and burnt incense to keep off the flies. Vinak took the carcass of the boar to my tent and began to butcher it. Slowly the camp took on a more civilized shape, with a ditch of sorts, not very deep, and a stockade on a continuous bank. If anything happened we could at least defend ourselves.

Nothing aroused us that night. I dined on roast pork and slept well. I had taken a last turn around the camp, inspecting the sentries, quite informally of course: there was no rigid discipline for me, not at my rank, for I was supreme commander. That would be for Crispinus. I could unbend, ask this man's name, comment on that one's medals, ask after another's foot that Whitey had stepped on two days before in the forest — anything to show humanity, a link with the people. I even took a last look at the guides, shackled to their post near the stone. Vinak had put them down a plate of scraps, as he did every night, and a bucket of water, uncovered, where they could reach it. The older man was in a bad way still, weeping silently. The younger man was sitting on his heels, his buttocks off the ground. He looked straight in front of him, his lips tight. They knew I was going to get the truth out of them first thing in the morning. I would find out why they had misled us, and which was the proper way. I left them to sweat on it.

I rose just before the sun, as always. I burnt my incense to the God, the Master of the Entrance. Then Trebius came to me.

'The most noble prefect must see this.'

I followed him to the side of the stone. The two guides were still fastened to their post.

They had gone willingly, and fasting. The scraps of pork and bread were still untouched in the pan. It was the younger man who had done the business. He had always had the air of superiority. The elder man was sitting upright, leaning against the post. He had been strangled with his chain. His eyes bulged in their sockets, his tongue lolled from a mouth too small for it, but his face was at peace. The younger man was on his knees. His head was bent forward, his hands clenched behind his back. He had drowned himself in the bucket of water.

'I have heard of slaves doing this,' I told Trebius. I forced myself to sound casual, as if it were something everyday and to be expected. 'I was not sure it could be done. How can a man hold himself so while he fights for breath?'

'There was neither pool nor well,' Drusus had come silently behind us. 'How else could he make a sacrifice?'

'This was no sacrifice,' I told him. 'There was no blood.'

Trebius beckoned the corporal of the guard, ordering him:

'Get this carrion out of here.'

The corporal drew his sword to cut off the heads and save the chain, but I stopped him.

'Do not profane this sanctuary. Do it in the wood.'

Half a dozen legionaries lifted the two bodies, still fastened together and carried them into the trees, out of sight, the way we had come. I watched them to make sure that they got clear, and then I went to the booth over the stone. It was as I thought. The heads were gone, and the gold collar. But there was something else, shining on the altar. I called for Achilles.

'What is that on top of the altar?'

He looked, and then laughed.

'Ah, I thought *she* wouldn't rob an old soldier,' he told me. With an easiness that sent shivers down my spine, he leant over the altar and picked up the gold coin. 'I wonder if she'll bring me back my wine ration?'

'You know this coin?'

'Oh, everybody in the Army knows this one, most noble Juvenal. There's my teeth marks. I picked it up out of a tomb in Thrace, and I've hung on to it ever since. I've wagered it two or three times, and I've always got it back the same throw and ten times as much again. That's why nobody who knows me will throw dice with me, and that's very troubling because gambling's one of my weak spots. So she's brought it back for me. That means more luck to come, seeing it was a kind of wager, me daring her to bring it like that. Haven't you had yours back, sir? That's hard luck, that is.'

'What were you doing last night? And what was that about your wine ration?'

'I was sleeping mostly,' he answered. He was one of those old soldiers who can always manage to arrange themselves some vital military duty which entails remaining very still, preferably horizontal, and concealed from all eyes, especially those of officers. 'But I did one watch as sentry of the Chapel.'

He knew he couldn't hide that. Trebius would know. But even so, sentry of the Chapel is the safest post to draw, because it's in the very middle of the camp.

'Did you see anyone enter the camp?'

'I never saw mortal soul, nor man nor woman, your most noble excellency.'

'You know what I mean. What did you see?'

He gulped, then decided he might as well tell me, feeling no doubt a bond with me since we had both seen the Goddess close.

'It was about halfway through my watch, the Goddess came by.'

'Why didn't you raise the alarm?'

'For a *Goddess*, sir?' He made it sound as if you might as well have raised an alarm for a puppy dog or a rain shower or the moon rising. 'She comes past me, and bows as she goes, to show she recognized me. So I presents my javelin, polite like, and I pours out my wine flask on the ground. She goes round the back of the Chapels, and then into this Chapel. Then she passes me and goes back to wherever it is she lives, Olympus or Ireland or wherever.'

I asked:

'How was she dressed?'

'Why, she was dressed exactly as she was the other night, only she was walking, sir, as stately as a great bird, an ostrich or a heron or something like that. She went by in the clouds of the moon.'

I knew what he meant. It had been a moonlit night, but with clouds scudding across that threw pools of blackness. I had used that light once myself for a night attack. I had had it used against me, too. I called Trebius. He assured me that nobody, nobody at all, could have penetrated the camp past his sentries. But I knew how the guard had been posted, and I thought I could tell where on our circuit I could have come over the stockade, picking my time, and with a couple of helpers. If it *had* been the Goddess, then Trebius might be right, for she would not have needed to scale walls.

Trebius began to get very eloquent about the iniquity of carrying wine on sentry-go. But I told him it was obviously divine providence, since if Achilles had had no offering, the Lady might have turned nasty, Goddesses being about as irrational as the product of the irrationality of Gods and of women. I only ordered that if such a divine appearance should happen again, then the General Alarm should be sounded, so that everyone might have an opportunity to turn out and worship and perhaps find a coin in his sandal. This luck-piece of Achilles was well known: there could not be many of the staters of Antigonus the One-Eyed in circulation, in mint condition apart from Achilles' toothmarks.

Then I gathered Crispinus, Camnas and Tarkul, as my senior officers, with the two standard bearers who would have to transmit the orders.

'We are going to stay here for three days at least. I want the ditch dug out to regulation width and depth, and the rampart properly finished off. Make up the stockade to a continuous fence. Get timbers squared off and build a standard gate house. If you haven't enough nails, Trebius, then it's time you learnt something about making joints — ask an *old* soldier.

'Camnas, you can spare one troop of horse to pull wood. Send one troop out into the woods, if you think it open enough, to look for game. If you can pick up another boar, it'll be better than nothing. If we can get the camp into shape today, we'll have a rest day tomorrow.'

'What will the men do on a rest day out here in the woods?' Crispinus asked. 'There's no wine shop, no women — we'll have a mutiny on our hands.'

No thanks to you if we don't, I thought. But aloud I told him:

'We'll hold regimental games. News gets around, lads. As soon as the Brits smell our smoke, they'll be here selling us barley beer and their wives like nobody's business.'

This, I thought, *will be my rest day. Tomorrow, with games and perhaps a market going, we officers would be run off our feet trying to stop the men selling the shirts off their backs and stealing them back again. Today I could play Agricola and sit back in my tent and make poetry. At intervals, I could stroll round and encourage the men, pointing out the beauties of the scenery.*

It was, at least, a fine day. The sky was arched across us from hill to hill, blue with hardly a cloud. The high ground was some way to the south, and the wooded valley stretched west. But to the north the stream was close to our camp wall, and it cut into the side of the hill which rose an opposing wall.

It was about noon when a messenger came riding out of the wood.

'Most noble prefect,' he addressed me. 'The noble Camnas presents his compliments and desires that you should send him men and packhorses, for he has found meat.'

I snapped my fingers.

'Trebius! Send him five men and three horses.'

'Oh, but we'll need a lot more than that,' the messenger told us, less ceremoniously. Cavalry are like that, continually reverting to low manners, which is why patricians find them unpleasant to serve with. I took the man's advice. We got together twenty packhorses, and the off-watch century. These men had been on sentry-go the night before and were now only wasting their time sleeping it off. I got on to Whitey, and followed the messenger into the jungle, ahead of the infantry, till it struck me that if anything went wrong someone would have to ride for help. I therefore prudently took the rear of the column.

When we reached Camnas we found he wasn't far, but he did need help. They had made a killing indeed. They had found a herd of wild cattle, not the little beasts the Brits keep for milk which they drink (while any civilized man knows it's only good for washing in or churning down into hair oil) but the big cattle of the woods. Camnas was an old hand, and his men weren't innocents either. They had found the herd upwind of them and working quietly they had built a funnel of thornbushes and twisted boughs. Then they had been able to urge the lot, very gently, into a corral, where our men had only to despatch the twenty head with spears. They were now cutting them up into convenient pieces for carrying. They really needed the horses. There were three bulls — one with horns as wide as a tall man's span. The cows were big as rhinoceroses, and there were suckling calves you could have ploughed a field with if you could find a plough strong enough. While the work was going on, I asked Camnas how he had found them.

'Now, that was funny. I was pushing through the brush over there, sniffing around a bit and looking for trails or droppings, and hoping for another boar, when I could have sworn I heard someone calling me. Talking to me.'

'A man talking to you?'

'More like a woman's voice, I thought. It was talking Latin with a bit of a northern accent, but quite distinct. It kept on saying, "Come on, soldier, this way, Roman." I wondered if we were being led into something. But I thought it better to stay quiet and say nothing disagreeable, so I didn't raise the alarm: Then the voice started to say, "That's right, boy, good boy, this way, meat, meat," as if I were a dog. I didn't like that, but I thought I'd better see what was up, and all of a sudden I saw the first of the big cows. I didn't listen for it after that.'

'The Goddess?' I asked him.

'Have your own guesses,' he told me. 'I only know it's steak for supper.'

'We must have crossed a boundary,' I told him, as we jogged back to camp. 'We've come from the hostile forest into the friendly country. We've come into the Goddess's own country.'

'But the guides?' he asked.

'They were our enemies. They must have been casting the spells that brought the bad weather. Then they came into the Goddess's country and she did for them. They killed themselves when they faced her.'

'That makes sense,' he agreed. The other officers thought so too. I invited them to supper, Crispinus and Drusus as well as Camnas and Tarkul. We ate well, and, for a change, in some kind of dignity. Usually, of course, the two Illyrians ate with their men, and Crispinus had his own cook and steward with him. Drusus looked after himself: I don't know what he ate. Tonight I had them all recline around my table. It was a pity we could not be nine, but that would have meant inviting centurions and squadron commanders, and they weren't used to formal company. It was kinder to leave them out.

We ate well. Not only for style. We ate the tongue of one of the bulls — not the biggest, because we put that head, complete with horns, on the altar stone for the Goddess. I burnt some of my own incense to her as well, because it was comforting to think that the Gods are the same whatever their nations. We ate the spare rib of the boar, and a couple of hares, and three ducks someone had picked up along the stream.

'We can forage here as we like,' I ruled.

'We could do with more beef,' said Tarkul. 'We're gorging ourselves on this fresh —'

'It could do with a couple of days' hanging,' Camnas grumbled. 'We ought to stay a few days.'

'We could lay in more if you can find it, and dry it over the fires. Then we could supplement the rations. If I can issue a pound of meat a day I can double our range on wheat alone.' That was a quartermaster's mind.

'Can we carry the honey?' Crispinus asked. 'Where did you get it?'

'Oh, Vinak found it, looking-for mushrooms,' I told him. 'Not so easy to move, but we'll try. We may have some empty wine jars.'

'There's no point in having full ones,' and Camnas leaned across the table and helped himself, which only went to show that for manners I might as well have stopped with Crispinus. Or perhaps with Drusus. He had been very quiet, as usual. Now he said:

'This, then, is the land of which the stories tell, where all is plenty. Here the fish wait to be lifted out of the water, and the game asks to be caught. They say there is a king's hall where the joints on the spit and the pies in the oven cry out, "Eat me!" and the ale jars shout, "Drink, drink me, please!" Surely, this is the border of the land of lost delights, the country of the strange meats, that so many of our people have sought in vain. At its centre is the cauldron of life that feeds us all, and beyond that a man may stand on the paunch of all the world. He that eats of that food shall never hunger again, and he that drinks of this wine jar shall never be thirsty in life.'

'Where is this land?' Camnas asked. 'I would like to hunt there.'

'South from here,' Drusus told him. 'Sure, are these not the hills of the legend? Somewhere here springs the Fountain of Youth. Oh, if we were but augurers enough to find it.'

I half expected Camnas to take offence at the suggestion that he was not the most efficient possible of all priests and interpreters of the haruspices. But he merely leaned forward in an interested way and asked:

'How do your priests tell the future?'

But before Drusus could answer — if indeed he would have answered — there was shouting outside. The soldiers had come about us, those who were sober; or at least those who were half sober and not full-to-bursting with beef and wine. They began to serenade us, as men often do. They described our social and political and sexual prospects and shortcomings in downright and straightforward terms. I learnt a great deal about myself that I had not known before, but I learnt even more about Crispinus, and, in passing, about Agricola. When there was a pause I answered with an improvisation I had prepared long ago for such an occasion. I described the sorry plight of the cavalry who were impotent except with their own mares, while the lucky infantry could satisfy mules, which was only fair, since none but mules could face up to their challenge. This made a good impression, especially on the infantry, who are simple souls, and we had no choice but to come out into the open air and drink our way around the camp.

There was such confusion that I was soon able to slip away unnoticed in the darkness and find my way back to my own tent. I was disturbed in stomach and in head as well as in my heart. My thoughts like the ceiling spun round and round. But I slept.

I dreamed. I dream seldom. But this night I dreamt that I was back in Aquin, and that I rode south from it towards the sun. I passed through the Campania, by way of vineyards and olive groves I knew. I ate hot risen bread, smeared with oil and garlic, at taverns where the wine flowed. There is no garlic in the north, nor oil, and the wine is bad through shaking as it travels. And wherever we stopped there were women. I had not realized how lonely I was for women, not having had one, that I could talk with, since I started up the Rhône. I could talk to them in my dream, and see them, real women with curly black hair and flashing eyes, not the everlasting light brown and red hair you see north of Lyons, and the strange light eyes like glass. I walked in the forum of Pompeii. I caressed the faun in my courtyard, and came out of my own door to lean my elbows on the marble-topped bars and drink the new season's wine from the sides of Monte Somma. And I saw my own love walk demure and meek and well guarded from the world. In a few months, I knew, I would be riding south from Rome, to take her to the unknotting of the girdle.

And then, suddenly, the Goddess came to me. I could have sworn that it was no dream, that she stood in my own tent, in the gloom, and I smelt her, the scent of meadow flowers and woodland blossom, like the scent of no woman on earth. She drove away my own home in the hot hard south, and my own promised one, and filled me with herself. She bent over me till I felt the warmth of her body. And I heard her voice and she called my name:

'Juvenal! Juvenal!'

The voice was clear, as I remembered it from the night in the wood. She shone in the darkness, in my dream, and lit up my tent, so that my armour gleamed on the pole. But I lay still, since that was the right thing to do with this Goddess. Then she began to whisper to me, low and clear. I do not know what language she used, but I understood all she said.

'Go south, Juvenal,' she told me. 'Go south! Down there is the land of lost delights, the country of strange masts. Go south, Juvenal, where all is dry and sunny, where never a man is cold, and hunger comes not. Go south, where the land is smooth and the soil deep on it, where there are no hills to climb, nor cruel stones to break a leg. South, Juvenal, go south, for there are all good things. Go south…'

She spoke on and on, for a long time. In the end she faded into the darkness, her voice sank into the whispering of the wind and the rustling of the leaves. Then I knew what I must do, and how I must keep it secret.

The morning was fine again. There had been no happenings in the night that anyone was willing to admit. This was the day I had promised for the Regimental Games, and though we had no amphitheatre, the legionaries pulled logs around to sit on, and built a platform to put my chair on, as Master of the Games. I sacrificed, and dedicated the Games to Caesar and to Janus and to the unknown God of the place. Or, as I thought, the Goddess.

We started with a march past of the whole force, horse and foot. Only Crispinus and Drusus, and a half-dozen men who were still too sick, were standing to watch them. The men had taken the dust covers off their shields, and now the rain had dried out from the leather they were easy enough to carry. They had fixed the plumes into their helmets. When the parade was over, I had shields stacked to make a bright pattern of colour about my seat. Then the men sat on their own logs, all except the pickets on the edge of the wood, and one troop Pepan took out to hunt. The men took off their helmets and unlaced their cuirasses, and settled at ease to watch the proceedings. If they missed a wine shop, nobody said anything about it.

Crispinus had arranged the programme. At least he could manage that. The infantrymen ran foot races, of different lengths and in varying equipment. There was long jumping and jumping over hurdles. We had no weights, so we used pieces of equipment. The winner of the high jump cleared the standard four-foot hurdle wearing his helmet and cuirass and carrying five shields, thus winning by two clear shields, a very creditable effort considering the weather of the previous few days.

But what the men really enjoyed, and what they tolerated the other events for, was the boxing and wrestling. Especially the boxing. I am not surprised that men, especially soldiers, like to watch other men cut each other to pieces with iron knuckle-dusters — don't we all enjoy seeing the gladiators in the circus every week? But there the fighters are slaves and have no choice. What I cannot understand is that men should enjoy doing this, battering at their fellows — their friends even — and being battered till they fall insensible. To apply violence when the Roman State requires it or when private policy makes it desirable, either personally or by proxy, may be a fitting occupation for a man of culture — how else have we ever recruited and trained our politicians and judges, our tax-collectors and our statesmen, the crowning glories of our civilization? But willingly to suffer violence is another thing. It is below the dignity of a gentleman and a scholar, certainly below that of a poet — who ever heard of a God who willingly suffered pain?

However, these contests are very useful in a camp. When all was over, several of our more unruly legionaries would be incapable of disturbing our peace again for some time to come. As long as they could still march and fight after a day or two to recover, it didn't matter how bruised and battered they looked. They didn't need teeth to eat their porridge.

Perhaps it was this natural transition from boxing to the loss of teeth that put it into their heads to argue about food. At the end of the Games, when by tradition the senior soldier present — not senior by rank but by years of iniquity — came up to the President and made the stilted speech of thanks, the President, being me, had to ask:

'And what last boon do the brave soldiery request?'

Now, he was supposed to put two requests, the first quite absurd, such as for immediate discharge for the whole legion with ten thousand pieces of gold per man, or 'if that can't be did', in the ungrammar proper to the occasion, some trivial and quite possible thing. Usually they would ask for a half-day free from inessential duties. But this time the senior soldier was Achilles. He came stamping up to me saluting as if he had two right arms, and demanding first, 'A hundred fine fat women of Delos to pass around from —' well, hand-to-hand was a polite way of putting it. But then, when he came to the alternative and possible request, his voice changed, and even he was serious.

'Most illustrious commander, we all beg you — we hear that you are going to reduce the food ration and give us meat instead.'

'But meat is food. We've got plenty of fresh meat for you.'

'It's not the same, sir. We live on what we always live on, wheat. And boiled properly, not made into cakes. I've nothing against meat, personally, not in its place — perhaps some nice roast pork in season, or a bit of beef after a sacrifice if they're giving it away, and then more for the holiness of it than for taste. Least of all for any good it does the body. Besides, there's the worms.'

'What worms?'

'Oh, we all know what worms, where I come from,' he told me confidentially. 'Folk who eat too much meat, they get worms inside them, and they rot away, all eaten up by the maggots of their own generating. They come to a painful end.'

'Nonsense,' I said, laughing at him.

'Nonsense,' said Crispinus, but he wasn't laughing. 'Get back to your duties. The rations are there, wheat and meat. Eat them!'

I didn't interfere. I let Crispinus carry on in his nice traditional patrician way putting the men straight on what the Army was about. He knew so much more than they did, having been a soldier now for nearly a year, and almost all that time in the Headquarters with Agricola learning how to be a general. And now he was out on campaign for the first time to tell us how well he had learnt it.

I had no call to say anything. I just sat there and watched the faces grow grimmer and longer and harder, as hard almost as Crispinus's. I waited till I was fairly sure that one of the rear rank men was going to throw a javelin at him, and I've seen that done before now. So I stood up then and sneezed, to make it lucky. That expensive course in elocution my father sent me to taught everything of possible use to an advocate except how to talk sense or use words as if they had a meaning. Sneezing was one of the most important subjects in the syllabus — two weeks spent on nothing else at all. It caught the men's attention, and they all made the proper responses, whatever they were in their own quarters of the Empire, bowing or snapping their fingers or calling on this God or that to spare me or to break my arms and my legs. So every man thought I was in his debt of politeness, which is a good start. And it broke Crispinus's train of thought, if he ever had one, and certainly ruined his current of speech, which was a wild and turgid stream. I reminded them:

'It's better than eating barley.' This caught their centres of worry, with its hints of punishment and disgrace. 'You all know how sensible it is to save food against emergency. That's all we're trying to do.'

'Not much good' (Achilles tried one last despairing grumble, so as not to lose his own credibility) 'if we're all rolling on the ground full of worms.'

'What we were hoping to do was to reduce the wheat ration by a quarter and serve out beef. But if you infantry feel so strongly —'

'We do,' shouted someone in the rear rank, but Achilles was silent, so I knew I'd got through.

'I will leave the infantry rations alone. I will ask the cavalry to take their issue half in corn and half in dried beef.'

'Give us the lot in meat, if you like,' someone shouted from the Illyrians. For a moment I felt like taking him at his word, but it would not have been the appropriate thing to do, since the infantry would not then have believed the cavalry were making sacrifices on their behalf. I continued:

'And as soon as the sick men are ready to march, and all the horses well again, we will make the shortest possible journey back to where we can get wheat.'

'Back to the Army!' came a chorus. I only smiled, for I knew who had been at them, and I promised:

'Tomorrow I will reconnoitre a way out of the valley.'

That night I dined again with my officers, breaking the usual custom yet again, on the game Pepan had brought back. I wanted to avoid being left alone with Crispinus: with company he could not be outspoken. I kept the conversation general, till we had finished. I found some delicacies in my own baggage

— a few figs and dates, dried apples. We felt that we had eaten well, even if it were only the jungle fare the men had been rejecting. Game may be a luxury for one meal, but as a diet it has its limitations.

'How will you go tomorrow?' asked Crispinus, when the wine was passing and Vinak alone was left to serve.

'I'll travel light,' I answered. 'I'll take…' I looked at them. 'I'll take you, Pepan, and Drusus.'

'I'll warn a troop for first light,' said Pepan.

'I said you, Pepan. And Drusus. The three of us. No more.'

He looked doubtful. I pressed him.

'How far south have you been?'

'Oh, south, if we're going south, that's fine. There's game down there you can't miss, the richest hunting grounds in the world.'

'How far have you been?'

'You don't need to go far. About two miles at most, and that's as far as you want to carry a quarter of beef across your saddle bow.'

'You've come to your senses, then,' and Crispinus laughed. 'I knew you'd do what I told you.'

I looked at Drusus. He showed a flicker of emotion; I caught a shadow of relief, perhaps triumph. That was enough. I asked Tarkul:

'You've been acting as camp commandant. How many still sick?'

He hadn't been expecting that question. We sent Vinak for the senior doctor, who came still carrying the urine pail he had been emptying. He reported perhaps one man who might find a day's march a strain tomorrow, but he'd be all right by the day after.

'Only a cold, sir,' he explained. 'Luckily, I had plenty of bats' dung for that. I'm nearly out of it, now, and if we can find a cave somewhere I'll take a chance to restock.'

'At dawn, then,' I told Pepan. 'Have the horses ready. We'll see how far the game run.'

4: THE MOORLAND

In the dawn, after sacrifices, the three of us rode south. Pepan was eager to show us how easy it was to pick up game. I was silent, the moment of union with Janus and the Unconquered Sun still hanging over my spirit. Pepan showed us tracks, dung, everywhere, that showed the presence of game. But it was not necessary even to look. The animals were everywhere around us as we moved through the brush in line, a spear's cast apart. The beasts passed near enough for us to smell: they even went between us, so they must have smelt us.

'Here,' Pepan called, not loudly by camp standards, but still loud enough to spoil real hunting. 'See how to get meat? You wanting beef, Velthre?'

I crossed Drusus to reach Pepan. We peered through the branches at the wild cattle. They in turn peered back, not disturbed. Their horns spread wide, their white hairs bristled on their hide.

'No,' I told him. 'How would we carry it back?'

But in my heart, I thought that this was no way to kill a bull. Down in Gaul, near the coasts of the sea, and in the hot towns of Spain, there they know how to worship the bull in death as well as in life. They drive the bull out of the hills into the town, on the steamy feast days. When the great beast of the woods comes into the treeless town, the game starts, the play that is a sacrifice. They run the bull through the crowded streets, follow him wherever he wants to go, wherever, crazed, he makes his will known.

Women throw stones at him, rattle their cooking pots. The boys throw knives at him, and dig pointed sticks into his shoulders. Men run in front of him, wave their cloaks in his face to make him rush at them: they dodge him, touch him, swing on his horns (or try to) and pull his tail. Where the bull voids himself, where the blood runs noble from his shoulders, or from his nose, on to the street, that is a lucky place. The value of a house may double for a touch of the bull on its step. And what starts the morning as a sport turns to a grim and solemn rite, as the beast takes the Godhead upon him, as he tosses men and gores them, and tramples them beneath him. Yet to be touched by the horns, like being touched by lightning, gives a morsel of the Godhead to the lucky man: it sets him apart as he limps away.

At the end, the beast, the dwelling of the God, comes always to the proper place, to his own temple. All wait silent at the killing stone in the square. There the priest of Jupiter the Looser of Bonds takes the long spear and goes naked to meet the bull. He strikes to the heart to let the Godhead free. After that, when the blood streams on the cobbles, when the God has died before us — why, then we eat him. What else to do but roast him on the spit and let every man partake of his flesh. Let the Gods have their blood, men need meat.

Oh, these bulls of the Island would have made such sport. But there was no town to run them in. The younger bulls spread out on the flanks. The cows and calves grazed safe in the centre. At the rear, we saw fleetingly the great king, with horns as wide as the yard-arm of a ship. We passed him in safety. He lifted his head to sniff at us, and I caught his scent. Yet the rankness was not a *bull* smell, the sweat was not bull scent. Then Pepan called, and I went to him.

'See!' he told me. 'Something new, and small enough to carry. You won't forbid me this?'

The ram stood quiet before us, not stirring. It had its horns tangled in the blackberries of the thicket, that had caught at us to tear our clothes and flesh, had held us back and kept us to the narrow path. Drusus dismounted, reached his hands among the brambles untouched, grasped the horns and turned back the head to leave the throat exposed.

'This I will have,' breathed Pepan. He drew his hunting knife. He gloatingly stropped it on the sole of his sandal, three strokes for the three Shades. I turned away while they were busy and slipped into the trees. The brush hid me in a dozen paces. I pushed Whitey forward, slowly, into a clearing. I spurred my horse on to the wall of wood that faced me, still defying me.

It was the edge of the jungle, which had walled us in on every side on the way. There was no entering it except by some door. And there was a door here, a narrow gateway through which men and horses might enter the wood, one by one, with the help of Janus. I rode to it. This was the way out of the valley, from the place where we were trapped in a prison of plenty. I knew that I had already passed the place of strange meats. What lay hidden within the southern forest?

I could not discover. He forbade me. If I had not expected him, and looked for him at every turning in the way, I might have passed by without seeing him. But I found him where he fell, for the Gods had granted him a good end so that he should not shame the Eagles. He had sought, at the last, an entrance, where Janus was. Or perhaps a way out? Seeing him, I knew there was no passage here for me.

There were only fragments now, mouldy leather and bleached bone. There was no shield, and from that, and from the set of the long-corrupted plume in his helmet, I knew him to be a centurion. His sword was in his scabbard, and a javelin had been slung over his shoulder. But in his hand he still held the staff of vine wood, that timber strange to the Island, which tells us all of Rome. And he held it wide, across the gate into the forest, to bar my way.

There was no question but that he must lie for ever where he died. I could make out the flakes of gilding, the paint, the embossing on the leather cuirass. The Unlucky Ninth, who else? So far had they come twenty years ago to find the Bridge of Sand. They had turned south as we were tempted south, and here in death they stayed our flight. Rome, in death, reminded me of my duty. There was a glint of gold within the skull. He had known death was coming, had prepared himself with Charon's fare underneath his tongue. He would long have crossed the river.

I poured for him the last of Rome, the wine from my flask. I turned back: Rome turned me back. My way north, too, seemed barred. The clearing rang with the clatter of weapons, and the grunts of those in combat. In the moment of my offering, the stags had come and assembled out of season to battle for the supremacy. In the centre of the space, the king stag of twenty points stood. One by one the young stags came against him, locked horns, thrust and pushed and were repulsed. But now I knew them for what they were. I took no notice. I did not attack the king. I did not linger to watch them. I did not even avoid them. I rode through the battle and refused the trial, for this judgement had no authority over me. I brushed aside the cobwebs that already hid the path I had come by, and I returned to the bramble bush.

Pepan had finished skinning and butchering the sheep, and had made the meat up into three parcels. Only Drusus looked pale, and worried, as if he were surprised to see me return. I said nothing, but took my share of the kill to ride north again through the bush. Pepan jerked his head at Drusus's small package.

'Funny man, that, only wanting the shoulder.'

'That is enough for me, I am alone.'

We passed the wild cattle again. Pepan was fascinated again by the herd king.

'I'll bring a section back for that one,' he grunted.

'And what glory will that bring you?' I asked him. 'You're too long away from your hunting youth. That bull is an ox.'

We came to the camp, and rode through the gate under the tower and the fighting platform. The officers and the bolder and lazier legionaries crowded around us. They asked:

'Did you find the land of plenty? Is there wheat there? Did you find the way back to the Army?'

I hadn't realized it before. These men depended on me. I was the one who knew, the man who could tell them things, where to go, what to do. It was at that moment that I was truly their commander, for the first and perhaps for the last time. I got up on the platform we had built for the Games. I waved my arms for silence. I got silence of a sort, a moderate stillness overlain with a varnish of murmurs, comments, questions. Before I could begin to speak, Crispinus asked:

'Is the road to the south open?'

'There's no road.' There were shouts of incredulous denial. 'There may have been one once, but it's blocked. There's jungle down there, thick jungle, like the stuff we came through.'

'We'll get through it again,' someone shouted.

'They can't beat us twice,' called another.

'We are not going south,' I bellowed. There was another catch in the hubbub, then the question again.

'Why not?'

'I watched the smoke of my sacrifice this morning, and I saw what Janus meant for us. I went south, and I found it is true. Listen! If we go south, what do we find?'

'Plenty,' was the anonymous answer.

'Aye, plenty. What's been happening to us here in this forest? Do they want us through? Ask yourselves. As long as we fought our way forward, they fought against us — whoever they are. The Island is full of magic. There's only one thing that can conquer magic, and that's Rome. So we conquered it, didn't we? We pushed through. Now, we come out here, and all of a sudden we're in a land of plenty. If it weren't for you lot wanting wheat, like true Romans, we could stay here forever. There's water, there's forage, there's food of a kind.'

'Aye, Brit food. All that game and such, they eats it more than bread.' I was sure it was Achilles.

'Yes, Brit food. Whoever are making the magic believe that if they offer us the kind of food they like we'll stay to eat it. And we'll go south after it. They've made it easy for us to go south, as long as we don't want to go fast. We mustn't do what they want. We'll do what they don't want. Tomorrow we'll go north, whatever they do to us. They're trying to keep us from the north, where the Bridge is and the wheat. We'll go there and see what they can do to stop us. I knew a merchant once who went to sea a lot. Sometimes if they stayed at sea too late into the autumn they'd be caught by the storms. Then, he told me, the safest thing to do was to turn the boat towards the sea and row into the wind. That was the only way to keep her afloat. So we'll turn into the wind, and go against the storms they bring down on us. But somehow I don't think there'll be any more storms. It was the guides who led us into this. They're gone, and good riddance. Let's show these magicians what a piece of Roman steel can do.'

That was fine, stirring stuff for them. They cheered me. But when I reached my tent the officers crowded round me, furious, and Crispinus the angriest of all.

'What have you done? Do you mean to take us up there into the wilderness? Nobody's been there before. We've no guides.'

'The last guides weren't all that much help,' I reminded him. 'We'll guide ourselves.'

'You know what lies to the north.'

'Only what we can all see, or guess. Over the stream we go up the hills. There's a track that runs slanting up the face, and the trees stop quite low. Up there it's too high for trees — it must be as high as the Alps. So it'll be like other places we've seen, open moorland and easy to march across. We must keep out of the jungle. Up there, it's cavalry country.'

'I'll go with that,' said Camnas. 'Look, if Crispinus is so eager to stay in this bush, why not leave him here?'

'Because I'm in command.' I would have thumped my table if it had been firm enough to bear it. 'We're all going north. Where's Drusus?'

'He was roasting a joint for his dinner, last I saw,' Tarkul told me,

'Then get him here. We don't know anything about the way north, but he may.'

Drusus was unhelpful. 'I only know the stories, and those not very well. They say that up there somewhere, on the high hills above the Bridge of Sand, the Gods live in an eagles' nest.'

'Who feeds them?' Tarkul was sarcastic. Drusus's voice rebuked him for his blasphemy.

'We do. With our sacrifices. You should know that.'

'But these low hills?' I asked him. 'And the country between here and the Bridge?'

'Eagles nest in high hills. So they say. Do you mean to go there?'

'We must. Those are my orders. If the Bridge of Sand lies past the gates of Hades, I will go there.'

'Alone?' Crispinus sneered.

But Drusus warned: 'If you go that way, you are lost. Far better go south, to the land of meats, or west to the sea. Have you not smelt the salt in the west wind?'

I shuddered. Men have no business on the sea, and I was concerned with finding a way of avoiding it, not of meeting it. I closed the meeting.

When I went to the Chapel in the morning, I wore my toga over my cuirass. The men were striking their tents and loading their packhorses. I had every man take an extra stake besides the one he had for tent pitching, and loaded the packhorses with posts to use on the treeless moors. I offered to Janus, the God of Setting Out. Then the men struck the Chapel. They had already packed the cavalry Chapel, leaving the stone in the open air. I offered more incense to the unknown God, and poured wine. I found Drusus at my elbow.

But this was not a Drusus I had ever seen before. He had always been a shadowy figure, shabby, self-effacing, apologetic. He always huddled into a grey cloak of vast age, much patched, over a tunic almost as old. But now — what was he wearing? I had never seen such a garment. It was a cloak, ankle-length, and simple to cut, but it blazed in green and white, and shimmered like the sun. It was made, all of it, from silk of Cos, or perhaps from Samos. Light as the gossamer it had once been, it must have lain hidden in his baggage all the time he was in the Island.

I looked from his cloak to his face. He was painted. His eyes were sunk into sockets of deep blue, and his mouth squared off. His cheeks were covered in intricate spirals of blue lines, and the images of snakes and dragons. As the men bustled about me, dragging unwilling horses to be loaded, casting earth on fires, uprooting stakes from the ramparts, they looked at him curiously. They had seen Brits painted like this before, and so had I. But not standing peaceable. Only running at them, swinging those absurd big swords of soft iron that bent, or lying dead after we had gone forward over them.

'Why?' I asked him. 'Why?'

He only answered, half chanting:

> *'Who seeks the castle of the Silver Giver,*
> *Who rests on the bank of the sea-salt river,*
> *Who leaves the Valley of the Standing Stone,*
> *For the eyrie that floats on clouds forever,*
> *Must find his own path, and travel alone.'*

'What does that mean?' I asked him. But there was a shouting from the men, who were pointing into the sky. I saw over me a cloud of heavy beating wings, threshing their way past till their clatter drowned our voices.

'Herons!' I shouted in triumph. 'Herons — cranes — our birds, flying north. What better omen do we need?'

'The Heron Queen,' breathed Drusus, 'married King Wren.'

And then it happened. Out of a clear sky, with no flash, no roll of noise, the thunderbolt came arcing like a slingshot. I saw it flame down, and cowered. But Drusus stood there, his arms spread wide to receive the gift of the Gods, in an attitude of prayer. It struck him over the left eye, mashing it into a bloody pulp of waters and grey brain. He could not truly be said to fall. He bent slightly forward, sank to his knees, then slowly laid his face on the ground.

Practically the whole camp had seen it. I shouted for a doctor, but it was some time before he came, since the doctors were all working filling in the pits where they emptied the night-soil pails, under the command of Achilles. He refused to release any of them from useful work without hearing from Trebius in person. But at last the senior doctor came. He rolled Drusus on to his back, with little ceremony, and fished with his fingers in the wound.

'Here, that's what did it. Act of God, you can't say no fairer than that, can you?'

It was a conical piece of stone, intricately spiralled, mirroring the spirals on Drusus's face. I wondered to see the doctor handle the sacred belemnite, a thunderbolt, so casually, but physicians seldom have the caution or moral sense of ordinary men.

'Stands to reason, you can't go monkeying with Gods the way this geezer did, and keep on for ever. They was bound to get him, one way or another.'

'Dealing with the Gods?' I queried.

'Oh, yes.' The doctor was proud of his inside knowledge. 'He was Agricola's soothsayer. He kept on rattling the bones and casting the future. I bet he didn't foresee this, though.'

'I'm not so sure,' I mused. 'He said some very strange things before he died.'

'Well, if he knew his end, he'll be worth opening. There'll be three livers inside that, not two, and the third one, if you dry it and grind it, is a sovereign cure for lycanthropy and a help in elephantiasis, so Galen says.'

'Which book does Galen say that in?' asked Crispinus, who was always making the point that he had a real library in his house, with, perhaps, even some of the works of Galen in it.

'Well, not in no book. It's sacred lore, handed down in the regiment since time immemorial, that is. What would I do with a book — I can't read. But I can write. I can write my name, see.' And he dipped his finger-end again into Drusus's blood and drew a double cross on the surface of the stone. Camnas grumbled:

'He'll be drawing fish next.'

I asked the general assembly (half the camp were standing idly watching):

'What do his people do? Do they burn or do they bury?'

'Oh, they burn, they burn sure,' said the doctor, too quickly, so I told him:

'You're a biased witness. You'd have to dig the grave. Anybody really *know*?'

Everyone could guess, but nobody had anything certain to tell me. I ordered:

'Two men, you and you, take him up. He was a sacrifice, that's how he saw himself. Lift him, carefully, onto the stone. Stretch him out on his back. That's it. What's that fallen to the ground?'

Someone handed it to me. It was a gold coin, not Roman, but a native piece. It was not very pure gold, and covered with a meaningless pattern of curves. It had fallen from Drusus's hand. I knew what it was for. I leaned over the body, avoiding the gaze of one sightless eye, the ruin of the other. I slipped the coin into his mouth. But my hand rested on his chest, and I felt under the cloak the edge of metal. I ran my hand over it. I had seen a living king wear a gold collar as a breastplate, and I had seen a dead king honoured with one. And this man? Was it true that he was a king's son out of Ireland? But he was not my enemy to spoil when I had killed him. I had not let the doctor open him. Why should I strip him? I folded the cloak around him, and crossed his hands upon his chest. I stepped away.

'Get the men into line,' I called to Trebius. 'We'll march at once.'

'That saves digging, anyway,' said Crispinus. 'The birds will bury the barbarian.'

I knew what would hurt him.

> *'Don't look so calm, Crispinus. Just think,*
> *That great pile of stone on the Appian way*
> *Won't be worth the money once you're inside it.*
> *Just think of the upkeep. Your heirs will have to establish*
> *Three slaves at the least just to keep it clean. Well?*
> *D'you think they'll waste that much of your money?*
> *They'll let it fall to pieces and you with it.*
> *Much better stay here, and get yourself burnt,*
> *Or eaten by scavenging bears — it's cheaper.'*

The Illyrians around thought this wonderful and roared with laughter, but Crispinus just shut up like a clam. If there's one thing a pure city-bred Roman holds more sacred than land or death, it's money. He won't stand flippant talk about it. But link money with death and remind them that they won't have any left to enjoy except the one obol under their tongue, and you've got a Roman tragedy.

We splashed across the river. We had no guide, so I led. The hillside was steep in front of us. The path we found had been made by sheep or hares. We had to scramble along it, the infantry sometimes on their hands and knees, weighed down by their packs. When we were well above the valley I stopped to look down. We had improved that place out of all recognition. There had been nothing at all when we arrived, except the Stone in the middle of the empty plain. No habitation, only the deep grass and the scattered bushes. Now the lines of our camp stood out on the green. Not the walls alone, though they were plain enough. We had set back the edge of the forest by at least fifty paces in every direction. There was a wide belt of jagged stumps all around. The grass was trodden flat or cut away everywhere, especially where we had held the games. You could tell the horse lines by the clouds of flies above the piles of dung. The tent lines were marked in the same way, only more clearly.

Around the blackened patches where the cooking fires had been lit were strewn bones, half-picked, the entrails of deer and cattle, the burnt scrapings from the bottoms of porridge kettles. Scraps and rags, the ends of broken harness, worn-out sandals, lay around for the Brits to pick up when they needed them: there was no sense in hoarding such trifles of manufacture which mean so much to the savages. Our tumbled ramparts strewed their raw earth across the plain, our ditches were already full of stagnant water with green scum already forming. No one could mistake it. Civilized men had been here. All we'd needed was a few tame pigs for scavenging. A pity we couldn't have stayed and made a real job of it. A pottery kiln, an iron furnace, later on a brick works — it would have made it all more urban. It would have destroyed that awful feeling of being at the mercy of the woods and whatever was in them.

Then I looked across the valley. I showed Crispinus. We could see the scrub and the deeper jungle beyond it. To the south, the land rose in a sheer face of rock, a precipice we could not have climbed even without the horses. Above it the moorland stretched in a level waste. *This side of the valley must look very like that*, I thought. But here and there along the other side, on the high land, there rose columns of smoke.

'It was as I thought,' I told Crispinus. 'There are the people who drove the game in to us. And in case deer weren't enough, they brought their cattle. Who ever heard of a wild bull gelded? And a wild sheep in the Island? Those people there on the hills were after us.'

'And Drusus? Was he part of this temptation?'

'Well, there he lies —' I began. But he didn't lie there any more. The stone was clearly to be seen, but there was nothing there, no splash of green silk. The Goddess had taken her offering. Or perhaps the men from the opposite hills had carried him away while we were climbing. What difference did it make? I turned to lead my force higher into the hills.

The land to the north was not entirely flat moorland, but hilly upland, the peaks rising high above narrow shallow valleys. But it was bare, with no woods for the Brits to hide in. There was nothing to watch us, not even leaves. By noon we had come a good way, so I stopped the column for a rest and a small issue of wine. It was then that Camnas came to me.

'We went through what Drusus had, down there. Not much, only a couple of tunics and some food, Brit stuff like oatcakes and smoked ham. Pepan took the horse — it was better than his. But in the little shelter Drusus built, with the rowan branches, I found —' and he just dropped it on the ground in front of me.

It was nothing very precious. The shoulder bone of a sheep. There was only one place he could have got it; this was the shoulder Pepan had given him yesterday in the wood. And it had been cooked, and more than cooked. It had been thrust into a hot fire till it cracked in a pattern of lines. What else do you do with a blade bone but bake it till it cracks and then read it? If you know how to read it.

I looked at Camnas.

'I don't know what it says,' he complained. 'I ought to. Bones, livers, they all ought to be the same. But not this one. None of the crack patterns are civilized ones at all. It just means nothing. Perhaps the Gods up here send their messages differently. Use a different alphabet, you might say.'

'They'd have to,' I agreed. 'One alphabet, one language.'

'But if there's anything we have in common with the Brits,' Camnas went on, 'it's that.'

He pointed to a crack running across the bone.

'That means?'

'With our Gods it means — death.'

'Whose death?'

'I don't know, without being able to understand the rest. I brought it along in case we found a Brit who could read it for us. It might be a trick worth learning.'

'I should say, at a guess' — I had to be cautious, you never know what God is taking notice — 'it was Drusus's death. That's what he came dressed for. They don't paint themselves that way simply for war, you know. They paint their faces because they may die in battle, and they want to face their Gods properly dressed.'

'It's unlucky, then,' Camnas said grudgingly. 'I'll leave it here. Time to move on.'

That first night we made camp on the open moorland. We tried to dig in, but the soil was thin, hardly a foot deep over the solid rock. We were just able to make a few deep holes to sink token stakes in to make ourselves think we had a palisade. The day had been fine, with blue sky and a warm sun. It was hardly worth while pitching the tents so I ordered that the men should sleep in their cloaks, on their tent leathers spread on the ground to keep out the damp. It proved cooler than I had expected, but I had a spare cloak, so I was quite warm. We gave the standards the dignity of their Chapel, which let me have shelter from the wind to burn the incense.

Next day it started very bright. We got moving very quickly. I had the column deployed to march as a square, with the packhorses in the centre and the cavalry spread out, troop by troop, ahead in a wide line, on the flanks and behind us in compact bodies, easy to control. I led the infantry riding with Crispinus. He began to make sarcastic remarks about being led into a trackless wilderness without knowing where we were going: the sheep track had faded out when we reached the top of the slope. I had had some time to think it over, so I was able to reel off at him:

> *'Out on the moors, riding a government horse,*
> *Fresh air on your face, getting up a fine appetite,*
> *Keeping good company, looking forward*
> *To a night of drinking with your friends —*
> *There's people in Rome would pay coined money for this,*
> *And you argue, Crispinus, when the Emperor pays you for it?'*

He didn't see the point. He only grumbled.

'And at the next stream we meet Cerberus? But it's better than some of the verses I've heard you make. It's almost pleasant to hear you cheerful again. Perhaps you'll listen to reason now.'

'I was frightened down there in the woods.' I had to confess it, if the change was so obvious.

'But you're not frightened up here?'

'I'm a cavalryman. Up here, I can see what's happening. Down in the jungle, I felt shut in. I was in a cage for the Brits to laugh at me and poke me with sticks, to make me angry before they turned me out in a circus to fight. They'd have the fun, but I'd die. It was as bad as being in Rome. There you can't see about you, and there's always someone to stab you in the back in an alley. I'm a countryman, I need space.'

'You'd better get used to the jungle,' Crispinus warned me. 'I felt at home there. My family have had long enough experience. We survive because we know there are no honest men. Bring us safe out of this, and you'll soon know all about Rome.'

'And if I don't bring it off, I won't have a political career. But, either way, I'll be dangerous, my lad. I know my own power.' I knew I was wrong confiding in him, but who else was there to talk to? Camnas wouldn't understand at all, and Tarkul thought of political life as shopkeeping with the cheating made legal. I didn't know what I wanted to say to Crispinus, only that I ought to sound menacing. 'Out of the wood and out in cavalry country, I can do anything.'

How little I could do now we were marching, I didn't like to think. I trotted forward to get myself halfway between the scouting line and the infantry. Vinak rode with me; the trumpeter followed close. I felt better now with nobody to talk to. I know these fits. They come when I have nothing to worry about. I looked up, and I realized the cause. It was clouding over. There was a wind off and on, from the west, bringing in a haze. Soon it was bringing in mist as well.

We stopped to rest at noon. I kept the conversation off the weather. Instead we let Pepan hold forth on the scarcity of game. He hadn't seen a mouse all day yet, he told us with many cavalry oaths.

'This is a real desert. We'd have done better for food if we'd stayed in the jungle, even if we'd gone west instead of south.'

'Nonsense,' I told him. 'A really alert man can find food anywhere.' I was feeling rather pleased with myself. I scattered a handful of mushrooms on the cloak I was sitting on. 'I've been picking these just here, while Vinak was getting out the wine.'

Vinak looked at them with a quizzical expression. He reached down and separated them swiftly into three piles.

'These, Velthre, you may eat,' he said, pointing to the smallest pile. 'They will taste very bad, except for this one. But you can eat.'

'If they taste bad, how about the others?'

'I am in this country a long time, Velthre. These,' and he indicated the next largest pile, 'they very bad, but taste good. You eat, Velthre, and you die. Not soon, but you will die.'

'And these?' I asked, pointing to the largest pile with by far the tastiest-looking fungi. None of these were mushrooms I had ever seen served at table in Italy, but they looked all right to me.

'These will not kill, Velthre. They will not kill at all. Better if they did. These destroy.' He gathered them up and threw them into the little fire he had kindled to warm the wine. A cloud of smoke rose into my face. I coughed and spluttered, and as I did so, the haze ahead of us cleared, and I saw standing up, far to the north, the blue jagged shapes of high mountains. But when the smoke cleared they were gone and the haze was around us again. Nevertheless, I had seen them clearly, and the eagles that circled over their slopes. I knew now where we were going. I stood, and everyone knew we were to move on. But I caught at Pepan's arm as he went towards his horse.

'What's that you're carrying?'

'Oh, the bone that Camnas found.' And he was gone before I could stop him, riding Drusus's horse out to catch up with the picket line. I pushed Whitey forward, ahead of Vinak and the trumpeter so that I could ride almost alone. I could listen here. There was nothing to hear except the sound of my own harness creaking, and the sound of Whitey's hooves through the grass. I didn't know what I was listening for till I heard it. I looked around, trying to see it, because this open windswept moor was no place for a hedgebird like a wren. I couldn't see it. Then overhead there was the beat of the wings of a heron, flying north. The men cheered it.

Now the wren had stopped ticking. There was another sound like it, a soft clicking and ticking far away. Someone was gathering for war, rattling spears on pots.

Well, that would be better than riding through this empty land. Man and beast had scattered in front of us, and stood well out of our way. If there was someone waiting for us, at least I would know what to do. I wondered if anyone else had heard it. But the men were riding in close pairs, talking to each other, sometimes singing. Only I was listening.

The haze was high, letting me see the pointed twin hills to the west, the stream below us in the valley, flowing north. The noise of the war call must have been an illusion. My depression left me as the sun came out.

The next moment, the cloud came down again, hiding the hilltops. It came dense around us, as it does in the hills. I lost sight of the horsemen riding in the wet mist ahead of me. Then it passed, lifting again. I waved Vinak forward to me, and he brought up the trumpeter. The wisp of cloud passed, and we could see the picket line again. Then I saw it happen.

There was the sound of a horn. And then they came down the hillside. First the stag, the royal stag of twenty points, huge and fast. The dogs were as fast at his heels, snapping and baying. If one had leaped at his throat, he would have been lost. But no dog could catch him. This was the Wild Hunt of the Gods. I would have known that even if I had not seen the huntsmen running fleet-footed, and the horse, white against the grey-green of the moor. And on the horse I saw her, all the legionaries saw her, and they shouted in worship of the Goddess crowned with gold, robed in silver.

I saw the whole hunt pass through the picket line from the rear, from my left to my right, the way of the sun if the sun ever travelled the north quarter of the sky. As she went through the line, she swept it up. Pepan and all his men struck spurs to their horses and went after her, after the stag, and yet were outpaced: the very huntsmen on foot passed them and went away ahead of them. The troop drew together into a dense clump of horsemen, riding hard, straight northward.

I turned to the trumpeter, who was leaning forward in his saddle, holding his horse back, watching my face for the word to go and join the hunt. But I was calm and unaffected. Whitey was content to walk. I snapped:

'Blow the Recall! Stop them!'

He looked about him blankly, not understanding. But the sound rang out. The troop ahead did not slacken rein, but went away from us faster and faster. I shouted to the trumpeter:

'Keep sounding! I'll catch them.'

I went forward myself at the trot, not too fast, since there was no knowing what that tussocky grass was like. There might be holes, snakes, anything to bring a horse down and break its leg. I could see the cluster of russet cloaks merging into the mist ahead. The men were shouting hunting cries. Someone was even blowing a horn. The greyness closed about them, and for a moment the hunting sounds continued. They stopped as if cut off by a knife. And after that a chorus of wails and screams, the most awful noise you ever heard from men or horses. Then ... nothing.

I rode forward, shouting:

'Pepan! Pepan!'

There was no answer. The mist swirled about me. I could hardly see the gleam of the trumpet at my right hand. Then I was brought to my senses. Whitey stopped short, digging in his heels. He was shivering under me. I didn't urge him. I dismounted, giving my reins to Vinak. I had a spear in my hand, an eight-foot lance, handy in open country if you meet a boar — or a man: not much use in woodland. I held it firmly and told the two men to stand fast. I looked down and saw hoofmarks in the turf. I stepped out, very daintily. One pace at a time. I held the lance at arm's length, the butt end in my palm, the point well in front of me. I walked forward step by step. From somewhere in front I could hear a faint moaning sound, very low, weak, horrible. I knew now what it means now to be blind. It means always to walk in fear. I had fear in my heart.

I pushed and prodded the ground in front of me. The moaning was clearer and weaker, nearer and yet far away. It was dying out. The spear point, after ten paces, touched nothing, stabbed only into empty air. I knew what this meant. I made one more step, and moved the spear around in an arc, from level with me on the extreme right to the extreme left. I felt nothing. I was standing on a promontory above — what?

I did not want to know. I turned my back to it. Looking down, I tried to pick up the hoofmarks. It was hard to see them, and yet I dared not lose them as I made my way back, step by step, exactly as I came. But then I heard the welcome trumpet blowing long blasts — to my left. I turned towards it

— and then stopped. Mist does strange things. The nymphs of the cloud snatch at trumpet notes and bend them, leading men astray. Now I had lost the hoofmarks. I grovelled and felt for them with my fingers. I thought I knew which way. Now I heard the trumpet again, to my right. So I kept on. The sound came again, and it seemed behind me. But I was kneeling before Whitey's feet, I'd seen him groomed too often not to know those hoofs. I stood and groped to touch Vinak.

'Shall I help you mount, Velthre?'

'No. Take Whitey's reins and make sure the trumpeter keeps hold of you. I'll lead us forward.'

It was lighter here, a little less misty. I could just make out the hoofmarks as I walked. Then I heard ahead of us, loud and welcome, the great bass horn, the legion's main trumpet. Another twenty paces, and I was with my soldiers.

'What have you done?' I asked Camnas.

'Halted, brought all the infantry in to form a square. Got the packhorses inside, and the flank parties close in.'

'Bring *all* the horses inside,' I ordered him. 'Lay out a camp. If you can't dig a proper ditch, just mark it and hammer the stakes in. Where's Crispinus?'

'Standing over there shivering. He's afraid of the fog. He's coming over now,'

Camnas had given all the orders. Crispinus asked me:

'What happened?'

'There's a cliff there, a big one. They went over. I can't hear anybody now. But there may be someone out there trying to find his way back. Where's the legionary horn-man? Start blowing. One long note every … oh, count a hundred between blasts, and make it regular. There's not much hope,' I added in a low voice for the two officers only to hear. 'They've all gone, I'm sure. Twenty-seven men, and one of them Pepan.'

There wasn't much else we could do. I couldn't have anyone move in that mist. For all I knew there was a thousand-foot drop all around us. I took the decision.

'We'll stay here for the night. It's bound to clear in the morning. Can we get this camp into a defensible state?'

'The stakes will go in for a fence.' Camnas had anticipated me. 'I've got Trebius seeing to it. There's enough timber to build a fighting platform over the gate. I've used all the tent poles, so we'll sleep rough again tonight.'

'What about supper, sir?' That was Trebius, thinking of his belly as usual like any infantryman.

'We've got enough firewood. Make it routine, except three-quarters wheatmeal all round, a quarter beef. Let the infantry go bargaining wheat for meat if they want to. Full issue of wine.'

Vinak had lit a separate fire for me, and without being invited the three officers joined me, bringing their plates. Tarkul had a full wineskin.

'Where's this from?' It was better than I'd tasted for a week.

'It's Pepan's — or it was.'

'Drinking a dead man's wine?' Crispinus didn't like it. Camnas laughed.

'Last time we did this, it *was* a party. Remember, Tarkul? That's the cavalry tradition, Crispinus.' Obviously, Camnas had started drinking well before the rest of us. 'Fill up the empty places, leave no empty couch and set up no memorials. Drink the dead man's wine, that's the best libation. Where d'you say he got this lot from, Tarkul?'

'Diced from some brand-new centurion, barely a year in the Second, came in as an optio, and no more experience than a legate. Name of Postumus.'

'Well, Pepan's subhumus now,' and Camnas laughed as if it were a great joke. He filled all the cups, and began the old cavalry song:

> *'The maggots crawl in under the skin,*
> *Groan, the old Groaner.*
> *The worm comes fat where the spear went thin,*
> *The old Groaner moans.'*

The Illyrians round us caught the tune, and joined in. They worked through it all, the twenty-three verses, one for each day of the Illyrian month. We cavalry officers joined in, but Crispinus like the rest of the infantry wrinkled his nose and talked of bad taste.

'After all,' he told us pompously, 'they have died for the Emperor and the Roman State. Should we not give them the debt of silence?'

'Immortal, are you?' I snarled at him. 'Are we never going to sing over you?'

He looked at me, not crediting it. I spoke direct:

> *'D'you think you'll never die yourself? Think of others.*
> *Remember Crito, with the crab that sucked out his vitals.*
> *Valerian, who fell of the ship coming over.*
> *Camillus split his gut, went vomiting blood and grounds.*
> *And Apicius, richest of all our crowd, was too showy.*
> *Caesar sent to him to open his wrists: he did so,*
> *And his wife. It all went under the hammer,*
> *Farms, pictures, furniture, a damned good cook.*
> *And that dark brown woman with the clutchy knees,*
> *He let me have her once or twice when I stayed the night.*
> *Caesar's enjoying her now, or at least her price.*
> *Don't patronize the dead, Crispinus — one's you.'*

Crispinus did not answer. He was very disinclined to stop drinking, sitting by Camnas but not saying anything except to ask for the wine jar.

I left them. The fog was dense. But it was different now. Fog in the day is one thing. The sun had gone down, somewhere beyond the mist. It was night out there in the Island. And it was thrice night here in our camp.

5: THE MIST

I made the rounds of the sentries. They were surprised to see me, but I found nothing to complain about. When I came to what for want of a better name I called the gate, I found the trumpeter there still blowing long, mournful, loud ... and counting ten, fifty, a hundred, and then blowing again. I checked, and I was surprised that they had a legionary who could count to a hundred. Still, I suppose they get all sorts, trade being so bad. I waited till he started counting again, and then I asked him:

'Have you had your supper?'

'... Seventeen ... eighteen ... no, sir, twenty...'

'Then stop blowing and stand down.'

'Twenty-five ... thank you, sir, twenty-six —'

'Stand down!' I shouted at him. 'Stop blowing! Put that damned thing away!'

He seemed to understand now, and wrapped the big horn in its leather case. I got up on the rickety platform over the gate and looked out south, into the dark. The mist was very still: mists in tales always swirl. There was no wind. The mist lay a damp sponge over us that a man couldn't walk into and couldn't push away. There was no chance of anyone out there finding us, whatever the trumpeter blew. Any men who were out there were gone for good. An end to twenty-seven men and their horses. And one of them Pepan. There was no one out there in the dark.

No one friendly. I could hear it, far away and faint, the rattling of spoons on cooking pots. They were coming for us, out of the mist. After the men came in on us, the women would follow. I'd seen it once, where a section had been cut off and killed to a man. It wasn't the killing that had made the nightmare, leaving men wounded but alive so that the women, the cauldron beaters, could get at them. It made me sick, and I am strong-stomached as a rule. I could hear the cooking pots now, and somewhere behind that the shrill howling of the women.

I wondered if the men could hear it. One look down, into the firelight, and I knew. The sentry below me was gripping his javelin as if it were a lifeline in the sea. The other men I could see were keeping very still. Most of them had their cuirasses on, and some were even wearing their helmets, which legionaries will never do unless they expect action. They were damping down their cooking fires without being told, as if it could have made us easier to see in that fog. I couldn't tell which way the noise came from. Perhaps it was over the cliff; perhaps they were working over what the rocks had left of Pepan.

I tried not to think of it. I tried to call up a picture of Aquin in the September heat, of my own house with the wine on my table, white and red, resined and sea-salted. I listened in my heart to the singers I'd like to have before dinner — and then I heard it blast at me, close to the fence in the mist. I'd never heard it before, but I knew from the old soldiers' stories. This was the war horn of a Brit king, ten feet, twenty feet long, they said, a bell mouth that would drink a man, a tube of beaten copper, a mouthpiece of cast bronze. The rim would be bound with gold, set with rubies and deep-patterned with red enamel. This was the horn blown only for battle. It was the horn that told of the death of kings, of the killing of men and the driving of cattle, of the gaining of glory and all good things, the taking of heads — and then I saw that the sound of the horn was making me think like a Brit.

I bit at my hand to rouse myself, I bawled for the trumpeter. But there was no need for orders. The men were falling in, the steady lines coming to attention in their places. They were stripped for the fight, no packs or plumes, just cuirass and shield and the pot on the head. Vinak came up the ladder with my bulls, but I sent him back down. There wasn't the strength to hold us both up there.

There had only been the one blast. It had made me tremble up there on the fighting platform. But where had it come from? The men could not agree on the direction. But I was armed, and now fighting promised I felt more confident. I half drew my sword and felt the keen edge: the steel spoke to me through my skin, of law and reason and all things Roman. I was five feet above the ground, but I felt as if I were floating in the clouds. Crispinus clambered up to me, and I let him stay, though I wondered when the gate would give way. Camnas stood below.

I knew how the men would be deployed. There would be one troop mounted ready to sweep out through the gate. One troop dismounted, standing by their horses' heads, ready to mount or to make a rush on foot. A third among the packhorses. And the fourth lying dead out there on the rocks. Two centuries of infantry lining the ramparts. One mixed up with the mounted troop to go out with them, the men holding to the horses' tails and the riders' knees to get a swing in the charge. One century just waiting. But all the infantry were alive.

The horn bellowed again. There was silence. Then again, as if all the bulls of the Island were bellowing at us. Now we knew.

'South,' was Gamnas's verdict. We all agreed. Then again:

'North-west,' he said. 'We are surrounded.'

'We have been surrounded ever since we came into the Island,' I reminded him. 'We have been encircled from the moment we crossed the Severn. The Empire is an island, Camnas, and it is the nature of civilization to be surrounded. The savages are all around us, across the Rhine and the Danube, and beyond the desert. They wait to break in, any time we forget that we are Romans and that we were born to keep them out. When there is just one legionary left alive on earth, with the barbarians hacking at him on every side, he will be no more surrounded than the Emperor is now, in the splendid centre of Rome. And if there be left only one barbarian alive on earth, one man not subject to us, only one man who does not keep the Roman law, then he surrounds us, however many we may be, and he is a threat to life and the Gods. Now, let the Outside try to break into the Centre. If they come from all four winds at us, we will hold them out.'

The horn blasted again. It was east of us, somewhere. But now we knew that this was the natural lot of the Legion, to stand in square with the savage world outside. I had awakened the knowledge that we were not threatened: the horn blew because we threatened it.

I crooked my finger to our own bass trumpeter. His horn was nothing very much compared with what must be outside. It was just the usual issue, third-rate copper beaten into a tube, a mouthpiece he'd carved himself out of a deer's leg bone. He set it to his lips and blew. The other signallers, infantry and cavalry, came into line, the high horns and the low, the straight and the curled. Pulena gave them the cues, moving the crane standard exactly as the drill-book ordained. They blew all the calls except the ones we might need to use now. They blew Rations and Sunrise, they blew Boot Issue and Town Curfew and Draw Flour. And last of all, in defiance of all regulations, but facing the standards as if in apology, they blew the splendour of Imperial Salute. There was no Emperor present, yet we blew it, and we heard Vespasian's voice in the brass, although we could not make out his words. So we no longer cared what the horns said outside.

For a time, the Brit horns were silent. I heard only, now and then, the cooking pots, very close and threatening. I tried to make out where in the dark they were. If only I could have seen anything at all, I'd have had a section rush them.

Of a sudden, I could see something. It was just light, visible light, there in the darkness of the mist, a sudden red glare of fire, hot and dazzling. It shone a moment, and died away. It didn't last long enough for us to see what we knew must be there, the cooking pots and the women coming in with their curved knives. The mist closed round us again. Then there was another burst of flame, green this time, along the east wall. It lasted barely a blink, but someone threw a javelin at it. Crispinus saw the spear arching up against the light. He shouted:

'Who threw that? Who threw a javelin? Tessarius, take that man's name. I'll have him flogged all over the camp in the morning. I gave no order to attack, I —'

'Be calm,' I told him. 'There is no need to set a bad example.'

'Calm?' he shouted at me. 'Be *calm*? I tell you I *am* calm!'

I raised my eyebrows. His shout had drawn all the men's attention, just in time for the next flare to show us up. It was enough, Camnas said loudly, to make a sphinx laugh, and laugh they did. We all laughed, at Crispinus and the lights and the mist and the darkness and at whatever it was out there.

For a long time after, there was nothing out there. No lights, no noise. I began to wonder if we'd laughed them away. I relaxed. I began even to count and wonder what would happen if I ordered the issue of a quarter ration of wine, which is what we usually do before action ... if there's time and if there is any wine. Then I did hear something. Not very close at first, but coming in at a good lick.

It was a mixture of sounds. Some of us had heard it before, some hadn't. There was the noise of hoofs, the feet of small Brit horses that hardly bend the grass. Perhaps three or four of them. And there were wheels running in well-greased trunnions, marking the wet earth with a deep channel, clinking on stones. And there was the noise of creaking, the flexing of a basket body on a light frame, yielding to the movement of the chariot. I reached for my bridle to mount before I remembered where I was. I found I had drawn my sword without willing it. The noise of the chariot, the jingling of the harness, the panting of the horses, faded away into oblivion, as we must all fade.

The men said nothing. Each of them was remembering for himself the tales about chariots. If the square broke, there wasn't much hope when they got amongst you. The charioteer had an advantage of height, like the horseman, but a firmer purchase to strike.

Silence for a time. Then, from the west, a scream, human, but a man and not a woman for all its high pitch. It was a scream of real agony. Just after that there was a dog howling. A big dog, with plenty of weight behind the sound, probably one of the hunting dogs they breed in the Island. And after the howling, a worrying sound, as if it were making the best of a big carcass, well boned, warm, new dead.

Then it came from the south. I saw it first because I stood so high. There was a glow in the sky, not like the brilliant light we had seen before, but more like the glow of a bush fire or the rising moon. But there was no moon. This light was red. It grew, covered the horizon from east to west, held steady. Then against the light we saw someone. It was a man, the shape of a man rather, looming over us, black against the red. In his hand he held a weapon, something huge and powerful. No shield would guard us against it. And from the south — the Illyrians said the south was the way of the dead. But then, to bring us back to sanity, the voice of Trebius was heard, stolid and stupid, swearing at some of the men on the north palisade who had turned their heads to see the show in the south.

The light died, the chariot passed again. The dogs barked, but more than one this time. Nearer, too. The following silence was more disturbing. We waited to hear what the next sound would be. The next sound was human.

I heard the voice. It came clear but low. Not a shout or a scream, but pitched in a quiet conversational tone, yet so that everyone could hear it as if it were meant for himself alone. It was like hearing a very good actor on a distant stage, soliloquizing while the villain eavesdrops.

'Roman, come out.'

It was not a challenging voice. It wheedled, coaxed, pleaded. It wasn't a warrior's voice, but something more evil. It sounded like the voice of someone who had been dead a month, with the throat half rotted away. It was a voice with the smell of corruption in it. It asked us in Latin, quite fluent and not halting or hesitating, but with a thick Brit accent, the sibilants hissed, the vowels nasal.

'Roman, come out here, come out to me. Come out, Roman, come and be killed.'

It wasn't really so inviting. Death in the daylight, in battle, is one thing, death in the foggy dark is another. Death alone has few attractions, even for Illyrians who talk about little else except how it is best to die, in battle or in your own bed or in someone else's.

The voice went on for a long time. It was very quiet and steady. It asked us, invited us, coaxed us.

'Come out, Roman, come and be killed, come out and fight.'

No one moved, or went out. No one wanted to at first. But the voice kept on, very reasonable and soothing. It was odd to hear a Brit voice talking such sense. I could not understand myself after a time why nobody went out. It seemed such a rational thing to do, to go out and fight a Brit. After all, that was what the Army had come to the Island for. And dying would save such a lot of bother. I knew it made sense.

'Come out, Roman, come out and fight,' the voice asked us. Such a little thing to do. I was on the point of saying that if nobody else wanted to, I'd go out myself, when the voice trailed off. The horns were blown again. The chariot came past us again, only closer this time. We could not only hear the horses panting, but we could tell from the breathing that there were the usual two men in the chariot, driver and spearman.

The light shone again in the south, and we saw the giant with his club, gross and hairy: we could fill in all the details behind the shadow. We'd fought men like that, often enough. And after the dog had howled again we heard the voice. But of course he'd lost his impetus and had to build up his credibility again. He worked hard at it, making his voice sweet as honey, smooth as oil — yet always it reeked of the long dead. When he had gone on for a long time, when I knew that I was not the only man who could be got ready to go out and fight, if only we had not found what he was doing to us, we heard another voice. It spoke the same oddly accented Latin, but it was different. This was a woman's voice.

'Romans won't come,' she said. 'Romans won't fight. They haven't got any. They won't fight.'

The man's voice took up the dialogue. It sounded a conversation between two reasonable people, the woman telling the man what he ought to know.

'They haven't got any strength?' he asked. 'The Romans haven't got any strength?'

'They've got strength,' she said. 'But it's wheat strength. They can't fight alone. They have to be in big crowds to fight. And it's day strength. They have to see each other.'

'Perhaps the Romans haven't got any blood. They can't fight without blood.'

'Romans have blood,' she told him patiently. 'I've spilt Roman blood. I've drunk Roman blood. It's gold, Roman blood, red-gold, and cold like a snake's blood. That's why they always hunt for gold, to make their blood. Come on out, Romans, let's see the colour of your blood! Let's drink your cold blood, Romans!'

'Perhaps they haven't got any balls?'

'Oh, yes, they've got balls, Romans have. I *know* they've got balls. I chew them off. I like them. The dogs like them, but I get them first.'

'Is that why they won't come? They're afraid of women. The Romans are afraid of women. Women-fearers, will you come out to fight?'

But that, I thought, is too near the truth to tempt anyone out to fight. The men know all that too well. More Romans have gone on fighting when outnumbered and desperate, more have turned the tide of a lost battle, through fear of savage women than have ever marched for Caesar and the Eagles. They'd have surrendered to a civilized enemy, where there was nothing worse in store for them than being beheaded, or perhaps merely being blinded and set to turn the mill. But not to savages who have their women handy. It's barbarian women who have conquered the world for Rome. Why do you think a legionary will go into battle without his cuirass, for speed, but will hardly walk a camp street without his kilt, boiled leather ribbed with bronze. To lie wounded out there when night falls and the women come out with their curved knives — oh, no, this wasn't the way to tempt the men out. They were afraid of women; they'd been taught this deliberately from the day they came into the Army, and they admitted it.

That was the wrong way to bring us out. She had broken her own spell and didn't know it. She talked on.

'No, it's a soul they haven't got. They've got no souls. Haven't you noticed, when you kill them, their ghosts don't stay in the Island to help each other? Their souls go down into the ground, and they always have gold to pay their Gods to let them through. They don't stay. Only our souls stay in the Island.'

'You can't fight without a soul. That's why they won't fight. No souls.'

'They won't even fight you.' Her voice was full of scorn. 'You, the runt of the litter, one eye and the left leg shorter than the right. Not even you. They're afraid to fight even you. Coward Romans. I'd like to see one of you try it.'

'Here!' It was Crispinus, the greenest man in the camp. 'Let me get down that ladder. I'll show her who've got souls around here.'

I grabbed his wrist. He might have been a rogue and a place-seeker, but he was full of whatever you get from half a thousand years of patrician pedigree and a moderately unblemished family name. Spirit, some call it, or honour or courage — I called it plain stupidity. Besides, every man in the camp could hear our private conversations. He struggled with me.

'I'll just take my sword and one of your light cavalry shields. I'll stalk him in the dark. I know how it's done.'

'It's the ones who know how it's done who usually can't do it.' The voices had ceased, we were having the horns again. 'Stand fast!' I shouted, to make sure that everyone did hear this, whatever the din outside. 'Any man who goes out there to fight shadows will be over the cliff in less time than it takes to wink. Stay inside, everybody.'

'Fight shadows?' Camnas wanted to argue. 'There must be nearly three thousand out there to defy us like that. And chariots. Anybody want to hamstring the horses? That's what they have those scythe blades for. There must be half a legion's worth against us.'

'How many, Crispinus?' I asked him, not to make him feel left out.

'Twenty thousand at least. They'd never come against us unless they outnumbered us at least a hundred to one. They know what we can really do. Twenty or thirty thousand.'

'Twenty,' I told them flatly. 'Not twenty thousand, but twenty. This is the Island of Magic. Every third Brit is a magician. They can bring things on us as easy as you like, fires and shadows. But when you touch them, they're not real. Nor are those shapes out there. Nor the voices.'

'But the chariots are real? And the war horns?'

I ignored Crispinus for a moment. I ordered:

'Stand the men down. They may sleep armed in their cloaks if it makes them feel better. Keep half a century on guard, another at two minutes' readiness. One troop ready to mount, but keep the weight off the horses' backs as long as we can.'

'We'll fight them in the morning, whatever the odds,' Camnas promised. He was as bad as Crispinus. I explained carefully:

'Twenty men, at most. And one woman. Even two people could do it all. They have a bull's horn to blow, and someone to run about fast with it. There are a brace of dogs on leashes, moving about and being teased with meat they aren't allowed to reach. They have a light cart: it needn't even be a chariot, but one of those little horsed barrows they bring the hay in with. Two of them speak Latin. One of them is a Druid — some kind of magician anyway. He made the fires and cast the shadows. If there are separate men to drive the cart and blow the horn and lead the dogs, there needn't be more than twenty. If there had been two thousand, they'd have rushed us in the fog. This fence wouldn't have been much use. Twenty thousand? Or even two thousand? How would they have come up on us with no noise? Anyway, there aren't that many savages left in the Island to fight. We mopped up their last army, the one from this part of the Island, back there at the Severn. You heard what I said? Stand the men down. Do it quietly, without trumpets or shouted orders. Don't give anything away to them outside. Pass the word from mouth to mouth. Just keep the main guard.'

'If you went out,' I could hear Trebius explaining heavily to some of the legionaries, boys on their first campaign who would be impressed with Agricola's Mural Crown, 'you'd never find them in the mist, not if there was only a score. They'd dodge you easy in the dark. Three turns in the mist, and how would you ever get back? But they'd find you all right. There's no point in fretting. Get some sleep.'

He was worth having. He knew a lot more about campaigning than Crispinus would ever learn. I stayed on the fighting platform, but I told Crispinus to turn in. He and the men might not actually sleep, but they'd at least get off their feet.

Silence now was worse than noise, darkness was worse than lights, chariots, bull horns, voices. They came again, as loud and menacing as before. But they were no longer frightening. These were only shadows. I took my standard from Vinak, and placed my hands on the heads of the bulls. I held Rome in my palms, and I could laugh at the noise of the twenty challenging our four hundred.

I stayed there all night. Sometimes I looked to the north, where was the Bridge of Sand. But mostly I looked south, to Italy and Rome and Aquin. I yearned towards them. Tomorrow the sun would rise there, hot and clear and hard. There would be no mist in Italy, no magic: nothing but truth and logic. There would be no debate about what was or was not, about what was seen and what appeared. Helios would rise, all dressed in warmth and wisdom, to voyage near the welcoming earth. Here in the Island, even at noon, he stayed far away. We were all but forgotten, but so long as we did not forget him, we were saved. I looked to the south and gave myself to him.

Beyond our fence of flimsy stakes the horns still brayed in fury. Hounds yelled, horses whinnied in the mist, now near, now far. Wheels rattled by. Spears rattled on cooking pots. Fires flared red and yellow and green. The shadows rose around us, the clubman, the stag, the serpent. All the magic of the Island was flung against us, but Rome still stood in her *gravitas*. I have seen worse shows in the theatre.

As the night went on, the intervals of silence grew longer, the horn blasts weaker. The dogs barked hoarser. The voices came again, but they were more flagrantly demanding, more scurrilous, angrier now even with each other. We did not hear them go, but we knew, down in our Roman blood, when they had left us.

When dawn was near, as I guessed, I went from the fighting platform to the Chapel of the Standards. One fire burnt before it, and a charcoal brazier also. Two men worked there. They took turn and turn about with the blowpipe and the pincers. Achilles and Trebius had almost finished their work of the night. The belemnite which had killed Drusus was now encased in silver. Without asking my permission, they mounted it between the horns of my bulls as a god-given crest.

That, I thought, is how to treat this magic Island. Take its weapons captive. There is no Goddess. We have been fooled by mere illusion. We knew the Island spawned mystery, but reason would defeat it. Janus and Jupiter, Helios and Diana, the clear lights of science would guide us to — safety? Death? Was not death a kind of safety? And was the magic Island more than a state of life-in-death, a middle way that was neither white nor black, neither light nor dark, a mist across the day of reason?

My mind told me that it ought to have been light. The day should long have broken. Perhaps the darkness of the night mist had changed to a deep grey, soft as the fur of a mole. But my eye told me there was no light, no sunrise. I wondered what I had done, that Apollo would not visit us. Was it the dead? We had paid them no sacrifice that he would recognize. The horses would be his, but would he realize this? We had made no wake, nor cried and cut our faces in mourning. That was the cavalry way. We had sinned, though; that was clear. One of the troubles about theology is that we never know what a sin is till we have committed it and the burden is on us. Therefore it will be many centuries before we have a clear and unambiguous code that someone can write down. We would just have to make our best guess. Certainly, I had not performed the worship of the Sun over the bodies. But we had recovered no bodies: we could not sacrifice till the sun came.

I made my own sacrifice. I laid aside my helmet and my breastplate, and stood before the standards barelegged in my tunic. I called for a Samian plate, my favourite, on which Vinak usually served me my wheatbread in the morning. I broke it before the standards. With one piece I sawed off a lock of my hair and threw it into the brazier. I gashed my forearms till they bled. I rubbed wood ash into the cuts on my arms so that it will remain till I rot. I mixed ash with my own blood to smear on my face.

Vinak brought my wheatcake and my warmed wine on a silver plate and in a silver cup. I crumbled the bread on to the ground, and I poured out the wine. Then I threw cup and plate into the single cooking fire, and watched them flex and warp.

Now I armed myself again. My dress cuirass was a good one, shaped to fit me well. The leather was gilded in all the most fashionable places and patterns. The bronze shoulder pieces were cast in a delicate relief of nymphs and satyrs alternating in pursuit; one pretty nymph on the left shoulder was scarred by a Brit sword in a skirmish in the spring before. I wore my parade greaves. My helmet was a compromise between show and practicality. Bronze is too heavy for daily wear, though best for ornament and protection. I had something lighter in stiff leather covered with copper, which takes paint well. I had the plume fitted in place.

Vinak wrapped my toga round me. He had spent the night pipeclaying it fresh. Unbidden, Trebius and Pulena had brought the men on parade. They too had fitted their plumes to their helmets and taken the covers from their shields. Such an emergency as we had demanded a show of reverence. I sprinkled the incense, and prayed aloud publicly to Caesar. And in silence I prayed to Janus.

There was some light now. The sun had risen somewhere beyond us. The mist was no longer pitch but grey silk. The bright colours and the gilding would have sparkled if there had been real light. But his face was hidden from us, Helios abhorred us, Apollo forbade us to sing. I knew what I must do, as commander. I offered myself.

I walked around the camp once, within the rampart, the way of the Sun, to show him how he must go. After that, I ordered:

'Light fires. Many fires, at each corner of the rampart and anywhere else convenient. Use all the firewood. Pull up the rampart stakes, and burn the tent poles. Make little suns everywhere to be our defence and to show the God the way.'

When the fires were alight, I went to them, and threw incense on each. All gums and perfumes come from the sunny lands where Apollo blesses the earth. The sweet scent hung in the windless air.

Now I went from the gate that faced south to the lands of the sun. I set out with my right foot and walked straight forward. When I heard the trumpet sound behind me I knew I was out of sight of my men. I shut my eyes, and spun myself round, on my heels, three times, and then more till I was giddy and did not know which way I faced. But when I opened my eyes I was careful not to stagger or to take a false step which might have angered the God.

I hooded myself in my toga and walked forward. I had come ten paces from the gate before I vanished, so thick was the mist. Now, at the eleventh step, I was not within the camp again. I thus knew the God had blessed me, and would at least allow me to make my offering, acceptable or not. As I went forward, at every third pace I stopped and made myself one with the God. After three times three times three steps, the number was complete. I drew my sword. I raised my arms in prayer, holding high the steel. I offered myself to Janus.

'Take me,' I told that God. 'Take me at this entering into the land of magic, into the place of death. Take me if it be thy will. Only spare the regiment. Let Rome's will be done.'

Then I thrust my sword into the ground. It did not go deep, merely half a hand's breadth into the thin soil over the firm rock. If it had fallen now all would have been lost, but the earth held it upright. Only a rational man would have known that. I was pitting true knowledge against the spells of the superstitious Island. I waited for a sign, but no sign came.

I left the sword and walked forward. I offered myself again. I took nine good steps into the mist, as if a centurion had me on the square with his pace-stick. At each step I expected to find no ground under me, to fall forward into empty space where my men had gone before. I willed myself not to look down as I strode. I hoped that I would neither struggle nor scream in weakness when the time came. To go reluctant might mean destruction to all my little force. The Gods do not accept grudging sacrifices.

After the ninth step, I stood still again. I drew the screen of my toga across my face. I waited. How long I waited I do not know. I emptied my mind of all thought, all knowledge, all emotion. I spoke with the God without sound, without words, without form and without meaning. At length I was at one with the God. I was the God. His presence was about me: I felt the wind of his breath on my hand.

A thousand years after I had entered into the Godhead, I heard a great noise. It was my soldiers, who were beating their scabbarded swords on their shields and hitting their cooking pots with entrenching tools and blowing horns as if they were Brits. At first I thought that this was merely their common sense in independent action. Such clamour is usually effective in driving away mists and fogs brought by harpies and other evil creatures. It settles an eclipse of the moon in a few minutes even if the light is quite extinguished. But then I heard them shout:

'Hail to the Unconquered Sun!'

I loosed the folds of my toga from about my face. The mist was no longer milk but pearl. Ahead, above, I looked to see the sun. There was still a thin scumbling of mist that let me look him full in the face. I saw Apollo, and I thanked the God.

Then I looked down before me. Another step and I would have been among the buzzard-eaten rags that had been Pepan and a score of others. I spoke their names, Cupis and Suphil, Thurinu and Daliak — the birds and beasts of the night still quarrelled over their feast. Man-flesh or horse-flesh, it was all one to them. We would not be able to reach them. The cliff face went down from me like a wall. That way they had gone; that way I was forbidden to follow. The God had not required it of me.

Behind me, men shouted praises. They called on him under a thousand different names, Phoebe and Apollo, Helios and Ra, Mithras and Shamas. For all men know him, and he knows all men to see them in their hearts.

I praised the God that only Romans know. I praised Janus that sees men from within as well as from without.

I walked the edge of the cliff. My officers came out to me. The men were sharing an extra issue of wine, so that they might pour their own libations. Gods are chancy beings, and if they do something for you and aren't rewarded at once, however meanly, they may remember it next time you ask them something. Camnas brought me my share, and I scattered it over the cliff on the wreck of the troop. Camnas spoke, in Illyrian, one of the first proverbs one gets off by heart learning the language:

> *'Death has set men's dwelling place in the abyss,*
> *But wine is given to us here and now.'*

For the first time I understood it. I looked beyond. The mist was scorching off the earth. Below us was a wide valley with a marsh in it. To our left, the west, the sea gleamed. To the north-east rose great mountains, reaching into the clouds. Their slopes were bare of trees, of grass even, rocky, sterile. But there was movement. Eagles circled. These were the abodes of the Gods, the eyrie, as fearsome as Mount Olympus. These mountains we had to pass to reach the Bridge of Sand.

To our left, to the north-west across the marsh, there was more level ground. The land rimmed the sea in a wide curve. Midway in the curve rose a round hill from the plain, smooth and bulging like the paunch of a pig. Beneath it rose a hundred pillars of grey smoke.

'There is a city,' Camnas breathed. 'At last, a place to sack!'

'You think it is a city?' I queried him. 'The Brits don't live in cities.'

'No.' Crispinus agreed with me — I wondered what he was angling for. 'They live in holes in the ground, or sleep in the lee of tufts of grass. The more civilized ones make themselves nests in the trees as apes do in Africa.'

'You've only seen Brits where we've taken over and resettled them,' Camnas corrected us. 'There's some places in the Island where they had real big towns before we came. Ah, they say Colchester was a fine place for loot when the first troops got there. The streets were paved with gold. That's a Brit city all right, and we'll be first there for the pickings. Look, that king we chased all up and down the Severn, he came from up this way. He must have had a city and a palace in it. We've got here before the Army — we may be rich for life.'

'If we live,' I reminded him. 'They'll defend it. You don't think we killed or captured *all* that king's army?'

'Well, that's what some of the prisoners were saying.' He wanted to argue, and I could see the greed in Crispinus' eyes too. But I had to be firm.

'We aren't going that way. We're going north-east, round the head of the marsh and past the base of the mountains. We're heading for the Bridge of Sand. That's orders. I'd like to have the first go at a Brit city as much as you, but there's no help for it. Is there?'

Camnas agreed that there wasn't any help for it, in the tone of a soldier who has spent his whole life obeying irrational orders. We returned to the camp. The men were packing up their tent bundles as best they could, having no poles to carry the baggage on. They made ugly and awkward packs, and slung them on their backs with ends of rope and bits of broken harness. I addressed them.

'About a mile along there' — and I pointed north-east — 'I can see a pathway down the mountainside. We can get down that way into the valley. Then we can make for the Bridge of Sand the most direct way. We don't need guides to show us where the food is — or the women, or the gold, do we? Who are we?'

The infantry chanted back at me:

> '*We are the Twentieth from the Rhine,*
> *Strongest and best of the fighting line.*'

'Next year,' I told them, 'you'll have a new cadence:

> "*We're the Twentieth from the Bridge of Sand
> We gave to Rome a wheat-rich land.*"

Last night, they had to try magic on us. They couldn't shake us, not an inch. We beat them. The way is open. Let's get down off this mountain as fast as we can! March!'

6: THE HILLSIDE

The wine helped us move. To save time later, Tarkul had served out the day's issue along with the libation wine for the sun, and the Illyrians had persuaded him to issue also the death-wine for Pepan's troop. And, of course, the dead men's issue had been handed out, since they wouldn't be struck off the ration strength till next quarter day. Therefore the movement out of camp was not entirely a model of military order. We straggled a good deal as we made our way to where a path came across the moorland and meandered down the face of the hill into the valley.

I rode out on the south flank. I knew what I was looking for, and I called Crispinus to see it when I found it. There were the tracks of a chariot plain in the grass — one chariot, or at least one pair of wheels. It had gone off to the south, the opposite way from us along the same path. I found one or two places where the dry grass tussocks were charred by fire. You could track the night visitors everywhere if you'd a mind to — see everything they'd done, how many they were — perhaps a score like I said. Small feet like so many Brits. But there were none on the hilltop, none over the moorland; nothing at all to worry about.

The men reached the place where the path went over the edge of the scarp. They rushed for it, centuries almost coming to blows for the honour of being the first unit off the hill and down to the road to the Bridge. The cavalry just rode through them. The packhorses were left to the last, in an untidy cluster almost untended.

The slope was fairly steep. The ground was bare near the path, but there were thickets only a few yards away and the hillside was strewn with rocks, some of them crags, the stuff of the mountain, but others boulders, rounded and smooth, resting on the bare clay.

The sun was hot on our backs. The men had mostly taken off their helmets and opened the necks of their cuirasses. They were struggling with their makeshift packs, sweating, but happy, because they had beaten the worst the magicians of the Island could bring against us. We were none of us on level ground when it came.

It was sudden and silent. There was no noise of horns or cooking pots this time. The first blows were almost unnoticed, even. The Brits had waited for us all the misty morning, knowing that there was only one way we could come, hoping that we would loosen our tight dressing and spread out. The sling stones landed among the last troop of cavalry, stinging the horses into madness, so that the first thing we knew was a stampede of frightened animals down through the infantry. They knocked men over and trampled on them. Then, volley after volley, very regular, as if there were someone beating time as an oarmaster does in a ship. Each volley came down on a different target.

There was no answering them. They had got us when our impetus was high, when we were already moving fast down the hill. They were above us and on both flanks. After the cavalry the infantry were the target. The shots were accurate, few were wasted; hardly a stone thudded into the earth without bouncing off a bare head or an arm, or off a horse's flank.

I pulled Whitey off the path and went slithering and scrambling down the slope to try to get the column into a formation to make a stand halfway down. But the men were running as fast as the horses, falling everywhere. I got past the packhorses, themselves now scattered along the path but closer together and altogether less disturbed than the men.

Then the second assault came. There were men and horses down everywhere, and hardly anybody could move freely. Into this were sent the boulders; the big round stones, half the size of a horse, were smooth and easy to move once you got them started. This was a long-planned ambush: the boulders were already loosened, so that if two men got behind one and pushed it would slide and then roll. There was no dodging them when they had gained some pace. They came down faster than a galloping horse, but not against the men. They rolled as if they were aimed slingshots into the solid mass of packhorses. The horses went down under them, the men leading the horses were crushed, and the stones went on, rolling over and over, into the infantry below. But it was not the horses or the men that came to my mind. I looked back, and saw the wheat sacks burst open, the grain blowing out over the mountainside. The wineskins spilled red over the grass. And still the slingstones slammed down, salvo after salvo, into us.

There was nothing to be done here. I kicked my heels into Whitey, and went on down the hill in a straight line over the steepest part. I prayed to Janus that Whitey would not put his foot in a hole or slip on a sliding stone, to leave me out on the hillside, waiting for the women. I took a stone on the thigh, but otherwise I was lucky. I was the first man on to level ground. I nearly pulled my arms out on Whitey's mouth in stopping. Most of the other horsemen went on past me, across the level ground to the edge of the marsh.

On the slope, all was confusion. Men were coming down at the run. They were dropping their packs, their helmets, even their shields. It was a rout of a particularly dreadful and senseless kind. For none of us had had more than a quick sight of an arm over a boulder, or a pale flash in a bush that might have been a face.

Some men were still trying to bring packhorses down. I could see Tarkul was trying to keep himself on his own horse, while pulling another behind him. Then a boulder came into them and both horses went down. When it had passed I saw that Tarkul had jumped free. He was bending over the packhorse, trying to dodge its hooves as it flailed in agony until he was able to cut its throat. Then he struggled to get part of the load away from the saddle. I shouted to him to leave it. I caught at a legionary who came running down towards me.

'Achilles! Get the officer down!'

'Help me with the bags, you fools,' Tarkul bawled at us, amid another shower of stones. 'This is the military chest. That's your pay and ration money for seventeen days.'

'Oh, Janus!' Achilles cried aloud, although he had not impressed me before as a particularly religious man. 'We can't leave the money. Bion! Shimshon! Here, make a tortoise!'

Achilles knelt on the ground, uphill of Tarkul, his shield held upright before him. Two, five, then a dozen legionaries ranked themselves around him. They massed their shields into a roof over Tarkul as he cut away the money bags. The stones rattled against good Roman leather. Tarkul slung the two bags over his shoulder; then, being a thrifty man, he got his own kitbag away from the horse he had been riding. Only after that did he come, heavy and careful, down the hillside. The tortoise came after him, the legionaries sheltering him without breaking step even though they were walking backwards and on bad ground.

I looked around me for a rallying point. Crispinus was sitting on the ground, holding his knee. Two of his centurions were bending attentively over their commander. The doctor was there, too; he had gone at once to one of the injured horses to collect hot dung for a poultice.

Trebius was standing in the open, a dent in his helmet, blood pouring over his face and left arm. I rode to him, 'Get up there, Trebius! Get the men up there, you idle good-for-nothing. Save the wheat, you fool, save the wheat!'

The sharp order brought him back to his senses. He lifted his standard into the air and shouted:

'Rally to the boar! Rally, Twentieth! Here, Achilles, right marker!'

It took a little time, but at last he had about sixty men in two ranks, a mixture from the different centuries. Other men were lying about on the ground, sobbing, examining their wounds, draining the remains of their wine issue, or just being sick. Then Trebius stood with them, looking up the hillside. Nobody was coming down any more — anybody up there now was staying. The green was scattered with cloaks. But nobody was actually attacking us down here with slingstones or boulders.

At that moment I found I had some cavalry again. Camnas was trying to rally the Illyrians, and he sent the first troop he had formed, perhaps fifty men, to me under Tarchies. I ordered him:

'Clear that scrub there, halfway up. Cover the footsloggers.'

He grimaced, and then conveyed my sense of urgency to his men. They did not seem entirely convinced. But he did a bit of persuading with his whip, and at last he got his men formed up in a line of sorts, but not very anxious to go. I looked at the infantry and worried about them, too. I decided to see what a battlefield speech would do for them. It's the standard procedure. I rode over to stand behind Trebius.

'Wild boars of Tuscany!' Because that was the name the regiment had always claimed, although some people just called them sons of sows. 'We have been treacherously attacked by men to whom we mean no harm. We offer them the blessings of Roman law, but they won't come and meet us face to face. That's the kind of brave fellows they are, hiding behind rocks and bushes to throw stones at us and kill defenceless animals. They won't stand up to us hand to hand. Just reach them, and then watch them run.' I changed my tone. 'That's all our food up there. We need it. The troopers will clear the enemy from our front, and then you bring the food down. I'll have another century up to cover you as you come down. That's all our wheat and wine — and if anybody tries to bring the wine back inside him I'll have the hide off his back. Now, show them what Romans can do.'

Trebius tried to start a cheer. Some of the legionaries made little noises of qualified assent. I waved Tarchies off and went over to where Crispinus was holding his knee. I asked him:

'Will you lead this charge?'

'Oh, I would if I could walk,' and he stayed sitting down. I caught at one of his centurions, and told him:

'Get another squad on to their feet and into line, if you have to beat every single man of them with your own fists.' I took him by the neck and pushed him the way he should go. He made a face and began to wander aimlessly round the men who were sitting or lying, watching the fun.

I returned to the scene of action. Tarchies had bunched most of his men on his left to hit the scrub hard. The rest were scattered in a screen across the hillside. They made about fifty yards up the slope, keeping their dressing quite well. They moved at the walk, the best a horse could do on that slope.

'Come on,' shouted Trebius. 'Can't trust the cavalry. Let's see if they can do their job. Get those shields up level. Be a walking wall. Keep in touch, edge to edge. Keep step, dress by the right. Take your time from me. Here, somebody who's not going, lend me your shield. Steady, don't rush, give them something to get frightened of as we come. Slo-o-w *march*!'

Trebius sheathed his sword, held his standard in his right hand and his shield in his left to give some cover against the stones. You could see he would end his career as a standard bearer. He wasn't officer material. An officer wouldn't have gone in front; he'd have stayed in the rear where he could control the shield wall.

Once Trebius was on to the hill, he realized that he was on the wrong heading. He wanted to turn them slightly to the right, not to follow the main body of cavalry. He should have given the order 'Right Wheel!' but under the unaccustomed pressures of being in action and in command he gave the Right Turn. Half the unit did what he said, and half what he meant. It happened as they reached the first piece of broken ground, which threw them out to start with. In a moment the shield wall was broken into a random crowd of arguing men, bumping into each other.

But worse was happening further up. While we had been re-forming, the slingers had worked their way further down the slope. Now the cavalry took the missiles in their backs, and the boulders rolled down again, into the main body, who turned and came down to their left. The confused horse came rushing down into the even more confused infantry. The slingers on our right opened up on the legionaries from behind and the flank. Horses and men were horribly mixed up, falling about on each other. And the stones never stopped falling. I thrust Whitey up the hill again, but before I reached the men, my horse was hit on the withers. He reared up, and although I clung to his neck, I was thrown. I rolled over, to avoid his trampling hooves, and the infantry did stamp over me as they came down. I followed them into the crowd, much bruised. I called to Pulena, who was mounted and had a good view:

'Find Trebius! Rally them again!'

Camnas had already got the rest of the horsemen into a fairly coherent group. He brought them to stand as a shield between us and the threatening hillside. The centurion was making some attempt to form a line. As usual, it was the men who'd gone up the first time who seemed readiest to try it again. They fell in, those who could still stand, alongside the sluggards. I went back to Crispinus, who was lying down with a big pad of dung on his knee.

'Come on. We've got to get back up the hill.'

'What's the use? We'll never face them.'

'Look! Count those!' The whole hillside now was covered with the rubbish of a battle. There were no end of horses with broken backs or legs. There were literally hundreds of brown shapes — the legionaries' packs made up inside their tent leathers. And a lot of things that had been men. 'There's food to bring down, as well as our comrades.'

'The men will have to take their chance. D'you want to kill more of them?'

There was no point in arguing here. I found Camnas putting some stuffing into the centurion. I felt I ought to put some stuffing into Camnas, just for morale, so I swore at both of them because the dressing wasn't straight and the cavalry were hanging back a bit.

'We've got to make it,' I ordered. 'Just hold the slingers engaged so we can salvage some of the food.'

Vinak brought me my own bulls, and a trooper rode up with Whitey. A legionary had caught at his bridle and stopped him, but the horse had bitten him in the shoulder, and there was another casualty. Pulena was holding the cranes as high as he could to be seen. Tarchies was up there somewhere on the hill, and his wine spilled there too, so we wouldn't be able to drink him safe into Hades tonight, unless we went back to find any unbroken jars. I said so, and some of the men agreed we ought to go, but not all, it depending on their respectability and their depth of religious feeling. The religious ones weren't convinced, but the rapscallions were just beginning to realize what had been left on the hill.

Getting the men into a better formation took time, since we were inventing a new combination of movements. We needed a strong front, and flank guards that trailed back ready to form square if they got behind us. And the horse behind the infantry this time, but spreading out on the flanks. It was a good improvisation, and a pity we never got a chance to try it out.

We were not yet in line for the attack when we began to hear noises. It was the cooking pots rattling, and knives being sharpened on stones. It was the screaming of angry old women. Nobody thought any more of the wheat or the wine. Nobody wanted to be left to add to the crowd lying groaning out there, waiting for the dark to come and the women with their blunt knives and their sharp chewing teeth. I felt everybody stiffen. It only needed a few stones from behind bushes that we had ridden through a few minutes before to start men thinking about running. I was going to try to hold them by pointing out how near the target was for this attack, but there was another noise. It was the slow beat of great wings. Over us went the herons, dozens of them. They came from the hills, and flew over us, over both sides in this strange fight where men died and never knew what struck them, into the north. They flew over the marsh, to be lost behind the clumps of trees and thickets of reeds.

That was the end. Horse and foot were glad to see this as an omen, a signal for flight. They abandoned all they had, and rushed to the edge of the marsh. I tried to stop them: flinging my arms wide, I shouted, I snatched at them, but they went. All of them. Even the standard bearers went, Trebius clinging to Pulena's saddle. And Crispinus no longer limped but ran like a hare. I was left alone on the hillside, with no company but the dead men and the dying, the crippled horses, the abandoned arms and the baggage. There was nothing else for it. I ran too.

The marsh was not a bare and open place. On the edge it was more like a wood with a wet base. The men did not run into it at random. The path came down the hill into the marsh. I followed it, along a trail of discarded cloaks and packs, querns and pots, even swords and javelins. And, worst of all, discarded men.

The path was hard and firm under us. Hooves rang first on gravel, and then on logs. We were on a causeway through the marsh, wide enough for a cart like the one that had run round us in the night. From my saddle I could look ahead to see most of my little command spread out in front of me. They were all moving fast, the cavalry fastest of all. I only wanted to keep up, but due to Whitey's inbred bad temper I managed to pass most of them. Many of the infantry dived off the causeway into the bog to avoid me, and I beat one or two troopers about the ears with the butt of my standard to persuade them that I deserved priority.

The band of marsh was barely a thousand paces across, but it seemed enough. It put a space between us and those awful stones cast by an enemy we could neither see nor touch. On firm open pasture ground I reined in my horse. Only a dozen troopers had emerged before me. They looked at me sheepishly. Making no mention of their flight, I ordered them to form a picket line to cover the way out of the marsh. The next man out was a trumpeter. He was a fool, because he still carried his trumpet when any sensible man would have thrown the heavy thing away. I had him stand at the end of the path blowing the Assembly, frequently.

I rode away from the wooded edge of the marsh till I could see the line of the hills over which we had come. There were fires burning up there now: probably they were cooking wheatbread and dried beef. To the north-east, almost to the east now, were the high jagged hills, the eagles flying around their peaks. The rounded hill was a little north of west, perhaps two miles away, with pillars of smoke rising from near it. But near at hand, less than five hundred paces, was something dark and threatening. Camnas joined me.

'You like the look of it?' I asked.

'I never like the look of any Brit fort. And that's a strong one.'

The grass-green ramparts were twice the height of a man. The gateway was towards us, with its hornwork curling out. There were no men on the wall, no fires sent up smoke from inside.

'We'll have to fight again. Get the men into ranks when they come out of the marsh,' I ordered Camnas. 'I'm going to reconnoitre.'

I rode slowly. Whitey was blown. Like all the horses, he was no longer capable of any other effort. He could just about carry me at the walk. I waved two of the pickets to fall in behind me. We went as far as the gate. No one challenged us.

We rode close under the earthwork and circled the camp, going with the sun, not forgetting him, though he was now dipping behind the rounded hill. The sky was flushed with gold and scarlet. We made the whole circuit. There was no other entrance. I stood again at the main gate and shouted. Birds rose up from within the walls, but there was no reply. It had the unmistakable air of an empty house.

I sent one of the pickets back to order Camnas to bring what men he had over to me. While we waited, I reflected that the remaining trooper and I were easy targets.

The troops came trudging wearily over to us. Camnas had about sixty horsemen with him, and nearly a hundred legionaries. Crispinus limped behind them. I walked forward with him and Camnas to hold a council of war closer to the gate where the soldiers would not hear.

'You really want an assault?' Camnas asked. 'Or do you want a demonstration and then a masking picket while we get some sleep?'

'I thought,' I told him, 'that we'd sleep better if we got inside.'

'We can't afford to get shut up inside there,' Crispinus objected. 'We'd be trapped.'

'We've been trapped since we crossed the Severn,' Tarkul corrected him, coming up just in time to hear him. 'I vote we try to take it.'

'And after that?' I asked.

'There was smoke over that way,' he explained. 'That means a city — people, anyway. And it means more. It means cloth — half of us have lost our cloaks. It means leather — most of us need new sandals, and some of the armour is in a bad way. We've got no tents to speak of. The horses must have a few days' rest. I vote we try to get inside.'

More men were straggling over from the marsh. I saw that some of them were practically naked. I ordered that the men who still had their shields and some armour should take the front rank. The others could come behind them and try to pick up weapons from the men who were killed. I made no secret but that we would have casualties. I told Tarkul to go back to the causeway and hold up any men who came through. If we were lost, they at least could get back into the swamp and hide.

Then I called for volunteers to lead the assault. I did not offer Crispinus the honour. I borrowed a shield and took the middle of the front rank myself. Achilles stepped forward to my right hand. One of my troopers, a fat man named Helluo, said grudgingly:

'If you'll fight on foot, Velthre, I suppose I may as well.'

He came to my left. A dozen more formed up behind us to push. The world was very silent, in the dusk. I felt as if I had not slept for a week, or eaten for longer. Nobody seemed very anxious to start, least of all me. When I could spin out the tying of sandals and the hitching of harness no longer, I ordered:

'Right. Let's have them, at the trot.'

That's the secret of an assault, or so they tell me. Get a steady pace, with weight enough to overrun anybody in the way, but not so fast that they don't think they have a better chance by running themselves. We had fifty paces to go from our start line to the entrance to the fort. We came by the hornwork, into a gloomy narrow corridor banked high above us. We went twenty paces, the second rank holding their shields over us, before the corridor doubled back on itself. Another twenty paces, and it turned again. Then a right angle, and we were inside the fort, wondering what was happening, not believing yet that we hadn't been attacked. Once inside, the rear-rank men fanned out so that we made a line of a dozen, ready for action.

But there was no action. There was nobody there. In the centre of the fort was an open space, almost a barrack square. Around the sides, wooden huts with thatched roofs, some free-standing, others set into the rampart. Just inside the gate, on each side, was a flight of stone steps leading to the wall walk. I told Helluo:

'Get up there and shout. Tell them all to come in.'

He made a face, as if he did not like climbing, but he went. We waited, watching the huts, till the first horsemen jingled in. Then we broke ranks and spread out to search the buildings.

And we found — what didn't we find! We found wheat, the most important thing, bags of it, and oats as well. In one hut there were hides, dozens of them, all tanned. There were billets of iron, and bags of charcoal. And even stacks of firewood stowed under the lean-to sheds. There was a well, with leather buckets and ropes. There was a pile of bronze cooking pots, all sizes. There was everything. But no people.

Tarkul brought the rest of the men in, and stared about him. He couldn't believe his luck.

'We're going to need this,' he told me. 'I've brought the picket in. If we light a fire on the rampart and have the trumpeter blow the rally occasionally, we should get any stragglers who are still alive.'

'How many have we got now?' I asked. I didn't really want to hear the answer, but it must come some time.

'A hundred and ten cavalry.'

'As many as that? I thought we lost more. They must have outnumbered us ten to one to inflict such casualties.'

I thought no such thing. There couldn't have been more of the Brits than we were ourselves. They had taken advantage of the high ground, and had used a diabolical weapon that ought to be outlawed, because it makes war too barbarous. But I had to say something to take the sting out of defeat. I looked to Crispinus.

'I've got a hundred and seventy-three. Fifty of those are hurt.'

I didn't ask him if it included himself. I was surprised that we had got off so lightly. Proportionately, the cavalry had done worse, but that was counting Pepan and his troop. Perhaps more would come in during the night. But Tarkul was reading off his tablets.

'We have eleven cooking pots and six handmills left, out of fifty-five of each. I can trace sixteen spades, three picks. There are forty-seven men without shields, seventeen without helmets...' He paused, '...and eleven without swords. There are two tents.'

'Never mind,' I told him, 'the men can sleep in these huts. Light the cooking fires, and serve out a full ration of wheat. Have we found any handmills? Good, they can have supper.'

The doctor appeared.

'I've dug the officers' latrines, sir, and put up a screen of that spare leather. Nice and handy to the well.'

'A good man, that doctor,' I told Crispinus. 'Can't you get him a promotion?'

'When we get back there's a retirement vacancy coming up as a loading number on a ballista in Three Cohort.' He seemed glad to talk of normal things as if action had been too much for him. Now Vinak was at my elbow.

'I found some wine, sir. In that end hut, the one with the heavy door. I thought they'd keep it secure. There's a lot of that apple wine for the troops. There's a ham for you, too.'

'What happened to my kit?'

'I saved one packhorse, sir. I've got all your personal stuff. But the horses with your tent bought it.'

'Then pitch one of the tents we've got left for me, and the other for the standards.'

'And the rest of us officers sleep in the open, I suppose?' Crispinus was getting back enough spirit to complain against me. I turned on him:

> *'It's all right for you, Crispinus, I know your tastes,*
> *Blond boys in the bath house, black litterbearers,*
> *And a silver jerry, nothing so common as pot.*
> *But I've a bronze pot on my head, with feathers,*
> *And a decurion called Niger shouts that he'll bring me in*
> *When it's dark and he can crawl out to me. I only hope*
> *He can get to me before the women. Some people*
> *Have to lie here with nothing to warm their white ribs,*
> *Sticking through a rusty cuirass, so that you in Rome*
> *Can keep your wolfhounds in the state they're accustomed to.'*

For a moment I thought he was going to hit me. Then he sneered back with my own line:

> *'Don't patronize the dead, Juvenal. One of them's you'*

I never thought he had the spirit. Or the memory. I went to the centre of the open space. In the twilight, the men were waiting to pitch the Chapel. I faced as near to the south as I could guess. I struck the heel of my bulls into the ground. The other two standards joined it on either side. This was now a Roman camp, whoever had built it. And we were now in Rome.

7: THE FEAST

'But why?' asked Crispinus. It was morning, and I had made my sacrifice. 'Why all this — food, iron, leather, even wool cloth, all left here in an empty fort? Is it a bait for us? Are we in a trap?'

I shook my head.

'This is the place they were trying to keep us from. It was what the Goddess said — we have passed everything, the rain and the mist, the flying stones and the falling mountains. Now we have reached the heart of the kingdom that guards the way to the magic Bridge. We have lost men, but we have beaten them.'

'But this is for an army. Tarkul keeps on finding more leather and iron. The cloth is enough to replace all the lost cloaks and the shirts too.'

'Of course. This is the base of an army. But the army is gone and will not return. We spent the whole of the spring and summer hunting this army, Crispinus, and we saw the last of it at that hill above the Severn. This is the booty of war.'

'And now?'

'Well, the king's city, his palace, his house, whatever you want to call it, must be somewhere near. The Brits don't live in their fortresses. All that smoke we saw — that's the place. So next, I will go to the palace and take possession of it in the name of Rome.'

'When do we set out?' he asked. I smiled at him, nicely, because he had to be told yet again that I was the commander, and besides the Goddess had made her prophecy about *me*.

'Oh, you can't go, with a limp — it would look very unlucky. And we can't afford to have both of us outside the camp at once. I will take the standards. But first we must offer. Vinak thinks he has found the King's private store room. There was very good wine there, in amphorae. And there were a few of these small jars with Greek seals, gilded. A choice vintage, obviously. Vinak! My toga!'

I robed myself and went to the Chapel. Vinak had set up the tripod, and my own incense had been in my baggage. I had offered once that morning, but now I sanctified the standards anew for a state visit. I broke the seal on the small jar and poured the wine into my last good piece of silver. It filled the cup. I spoke the right words, in Latin to the boar of the Twentieth, in Illyrian to the cranes, and in Greek, the only language for men of culture, to my bulls. Then I made myself one with the Gods in the normal way. I drank half the wine at one gulp; the rest I poured on to the glowing charcoal. The wine was strange tasting, not resinated, for the Brits have strange ideas and don't add anything to their drinks. But it was recognizably a good wine. As I slowly spilled it on to the fire, it burnt in strange blue flames and the scent overpowered the incense. I smashed the jar with the hilt of my sword. Then I mounted Whitey. So long as we did not have to ride far or fast he would do today.

Going out of the gate, Trebius took the lead since the legion is always senior. He carried his boar over his shoulder. Pulena with the cranes rode on my right, Vinak with my bulls on my left. Twenty legionaries, ten troopers, the fittest to ride or march, came behind. Achilles was there, of course.

We rode towards the edge of the wood that surrounded the round hill. There was a well-trodden path, from the gate into the brush. We followed it.

He appeared at the edge of the wood. Whether he was there all the time, or whether he came out of the wood, I do not know. We only saw him there, twenty paces in front of us, barring the way. He was the first man we had met since we crossed the Severn. We had come through empty desert, and at last we met a man. His beard was long and white, his tunic of green linen, embroidered with silver wire fine as hairs. And his head was shaved across from ear to ear.

By this I knew him to be a Druid, though I had never seen one before. I felt it would make matters a little delicate if I obeyed standing orders and killed him on sight. The men, I sensed, felt the same. I leaned down to him and shouted:

'Where king? Where? You take king, fast-fast!'

He looked up at me with frosty hard blue eyes. Then he answered in a voice full of mild reasonable reproach, as if I had made some natural mistake.

'It iss no need there iss for you to be shouting so loud. It iss still hearing well that I am, and it iss all my other ssensssess I am having. Follow me, if it iss that iss what you are wishing, and in the villa if you pleasse tell uss what you have come for.'

His Latin had the usual Brit distortions, but beneath it was an unmistakable Mantuan accent. I tried not to laugh at it, or at the idea of calling one of those Brit houses, all wood and turf, a villa. Or at anyone not knowing what Rome had come for. I ordered him.

'Walk on before us.'

He took Whitey's bridle. So Trebius, with his standard, walked on the other side of me. We said nothing as we followed a winding path, well beaten out, and wide enough for us to walk three abreast. It was made, I guessed, for a chariot, or perhaps a farm cart. The bushes were close about us, a dark grove of tall trees ahead. As I rode, I began to hear, coming on us so softly that I could not name the moment when it began, the sound I had dreaded, the sound of the wren. Now, I knew, we were in the Wren King's territory. And no other bird flew here, except the herons, circling overhead.

Therefore I felt no fear when we turned a corner and faced the edge of the deep wood. On either side of the roadway stretched a row of stakes, twice the height of a man. They stood vertical from the pits into which they were sunk. On each from pegs of wood hung heads, many heads to each post. Some were well fleshed and not long dead, others were bare and smooth, brown and green and mossed and rotting. I had heard of places where the Brits did this, and tales passed that the Gauls had done it before Caesar came. But I had never heard of one like this. For not all the heads were the heads of men: some, notably the heads that topped each pole in honour, were the heads of horses.

And now I knew where I was. This was the entrance to a temple. For the Brits, and the Gauls, and I suppose the Irish, do not build temples simply where they wish to worship as civilized men do, convenient to their cities and their houses. They have them where the Gods wish them to be, and then go to dwell near the sacred places. They worship their Gods where they have seen their epiphanies. Some of these epiphanies are at deep pools, and at the dark and still places at the bends of rivers; as where the Goddess Sabrina herself hovers above her own waters, and is most present when she brings the great wave on her feast. Others are at rocks and stones, especially at the wanderers as we had seen. Others are at great peaks and especially at the eagles' nest that frowned on us as we stood there. But most epiphanies have been in a grove or a deep wood, and had I been a Brit I would have built a shrine where the Goddess spoke to me in the thunder, and then made myself a house there and tended the shrine for ever. All this I came to know later. But I already guessed that this temple was a wood, or this wood a temple. The Goddess worshipped here was one we all knew, or at least had heard of. Here had appeared Epona, the Great Mare.

My guide halted. He reached into his pouch and took out a handful of wheat to scatter on the ground before the gate pillars. He turned to me, challenging. But I was prepared. To each of the gate pillars I cast a gold aureus. But not new minted. I thought it appropriate to give them what I had by chance, or perhaps not by chance, money of Caligula, lover of horses, lately deified. It was not my money, but came from the military chest. After all I was on duty and had an imprest. But in the gateway of Epona I made an offering in my heart to the God of Gates.

Then I showed my manners. I dismounted. I could not ride a horse, certainly not a whole stallion like Whitey, within the precincts of the Horse Mother. I handed the reins to Vinak, took my bulls from him and walked forward to the threshold. Trebius followed me, and then his shadow vanished from the corner of my eye. I looked back, and perhaps it was that that caused the disaster. The old man stood in the way behind me, barring the gate with his outspread hands. Trebius shifted the boar to his left hand, drew his sword.

'Wait,' I ordered him. The old man turned his back carelessly on the steel and spoke to me.

'You must come here alone.'

'And give myself into your hands?'

'You think we would harm you — here? You have an army at your back to follow and avenge your every hurt. If we took you, these soldiers would hold it an affront against their Eagles, and would take no notice of anything we threatened to do to you. They would just burst in here regardless of curses, and take you back — alive or dead.'

It was true. There was little danger that my head would decorate these posts until I had at least walked in and out again. I felt that a gesture of assent was needed. I fumbled beneath my toga and loosened my sword belt. I laid it on the ground before the gate pillars.

'Go back,' I ordered Trebius. 'Let all the routine of the camp go on. Let no one come to seek me even if I stay all night — or several nights. I'm sure that if harm comes to me, you will hear about it. I scream well, and they are bound to flaunt it in your faces. As long as you hear nothing, I am safe.'

Trebius didn't like it, but it was an order. He saluted. I passed between the pillars and entered into the middle of the wood. The old man went in front of me.

If I were a poet, I mean a real poet, a Vergil or a Licinius, I could describe that walk through the wood of Epona. It was not a wild wood. The trees were not there by chance. There were seven trees and seven only, again and again. The birch and the willow, the holly and the hazel, the oak and the quince and the alder. The dead pillars stood between the living trees. The horse skulls, the man skulls, looked down on me, row by row. Battered helmets, scarred shields hung on the pegs and were heaped at the feet of the pillars. Most were British, high pointed with wide spreading wings or horns. The shields were faced with copper, patterned in red enamel, set with jewels, rubies and garnets. Man-high, they would have hidden the driver of a chariot and kept his spearman from harm. The chariots were here also, the frames hung up on the pillars, the wheels leaning against them.

Many of the pillars were very old. In some places they had rotted through and fallen, scattering their fruits of ancient wars to breed new ones. But some pillars were new, their wood gleaming white. These helmets were rounded, with cheek pieces hinged down, the plumes still in their sockets. The shields were of leather over limewood. I did not look to see whence these trees took their burden. I only asked Janus to preserve the numbers Two and Six and Twenty. Nine was beyond Divine help, being already accursed.

We passed through the temple and came out of the wood through the western gates. We were below the side of the rounded hill which towered above us, three times the height of the Capitol. Below it, I saw the villa, as my guide had called it.

It might have been worthy of the name. There was in its centre a great round hall, a hundred feet across. The roof rose in Brit manner to a point of thatch and smoke came out of the point. On the turf of the roof grew not little tufts of grass as we usually see, or even small bushes, but young rowan trees in berry.

There were other smaller huts between us and the hall. The path went among them. There were people here, the first I had seen for many weeks. Villagers do not stay when the Army comes. Horses were tethered to posts and stakes. Women were busying for milking. Hens looked for grain, and pigs rooted among the garbage. It might have been Rome itself, that sunny morning, with all the bustle of life and civilized traffic. Well, perhaps not Rome, but any small town in Italy. Except this — the village was fenced off with a palisade, and the posts held, here and there, their burden of skulls, with empty eye sockets and grinning teeth.

My guide stopped. He turned to me, and pointed to the hall. He told me:

'From here you go alone.'

It was obvious. He was a holy man, a priest of the woods, and he might not enter a dwelling of man. His hand shone in the sunlight as he gestured the way I should take. I bowed to him, and laid my bull standard across my shoulder. As I came nearer the hall, it seemed vaster than before. It looked more like a great hill itself than like a building. The timbers where I could see them were green with age. It was a hundred times greater than the little huts before it where people lived and worked, and were too self-concerned to look at me.

The women turned their handmills. Men were threshing, or stood in smithies, beating out iron on glowing charcoal, hammering good steel blades from bog iron. Children followed the hens and gathered eggs. They took no notice of me, not even the little ones. They did not raise their eyes to watch me go by. I might as well have been in Rome. The dress was not so very different. What can a poor man do with his little parcel of wool, all he can afford, but make himself a loincloth and perhaps a tunic. If it is cold you may see him with a cloak, but with normal luck, which is to say bad luck, he has to huddle in whatever shelter he can find, or get wet and cold.

My toga certainly marked me out as an intruder, but so it would have done almost anywhere within the Empire, even in Rome. Nobody in a proletarian quarter would have given a man in a toga a second glance, merely noting that it was some official on business, a tax-gatherer, or a lawyer going to see a client — or a victim — straight from court. I might as well have been in Rome. Or dead.

No more did I look around me. These people were like any crowd of the poor within the Empire. Surely the fact that I was here showed that they were within the Empire now. The mighty Caesar and the most noble Agricola and a whole host of contractors for taxes and labour and salt were eager and anxious to take all these peasants' troubles on their own shoulders — for a consideration of ninety per cent of the profits and no liability for the losses. I felt familiar. I was not far in my mind — as I was never far — from Aquin.

I passed through the houses. Alone, I kept my eyes on the door of the hall that faced east to the rising sun and to the chilling winds. I had not realized that the space between the houses and the hall was so wide, or that the building itself was so far from the grove. It did not seem to get any nearer as I walked towards it, it merely looked bigger. I passed through the opposite gate of the village and saw the skulls. Then I came to a new barrier. A furrow was ploughed, the earth fresh turned and moist, between the town and the hall.

I was not so ill-mannered or so irreligious as to step over the furrow. I saw a little to the right of my direct line of approach a gap in the line of broken ground. As I turned towards it I saw suddenly that there was a fire burning on the ground within the furrow. Over the fire was a tripod of straight boughs, roughly trimmed, the sap still flowing.

From the tripod by a scrap of iron chain hung a cooking pot blackened with long use. And suddenly, again, I was aware that by the fire there sat three women.

I looked across the fire at them, not wishing to cross the furrow without their permission. The smoke from the fire blew into my eyes, and the smell was sweet, like that of a high-quality incense or the wine I had burnt before the standards that morning. I blinked with tears, and tried to count the women, or even to see them clear. They sat still and looked at me in silence. I regarded them with such benignity as I could muster, being out of breath and wanting to sneeze and not daring to for the danger of bad luck and wanting to rub my eyes and not risking that for the sake of my dignity, and much hampered by having my bulls to hold, when keeping a toga together gives full occupation to one hand and hampers the other. I had to be careful, too, not to get a spark from the spitting logs on to my toga, since then poor Vinak would have to pipeclay it fresh, and he would be careful to let me know how much extra time he had put in on that.

The women, as far as I could see them, were dressed in dirty rags: under the dirt, the cloth might have been as black as were their sooty hands. Their feet were bare. They did not look at me, so after I had looked my fill at them — and this did not take very long since none of them was, to put it mildly, a beauty, or even so fresh as to arouse my lust after a week in the forest — I made a move to walk around them. I went, of course, to the right of the fire, it being dead in my way. Therefore it was the woman to the right of the fire, not the one to the left or the one directly across it, who spoke to me. She used quite accurate if somewhat pedantic Latin, with some quantities that might have come back north with Brennus.

'You have come far, traveller?'

'I have come far,' I answered, and then out of prudence rather than out of genuine respect I added, 'Mother.' This seemed to amuse her, because she cackled with laughter. And then she hazarded:

'From across the treacherous waters, and mountains hard as glass?'

'Across salt waters and the unmelting snows,' I agreed. 'Through forests that tore the flesh from my bones, beneath rocks that roll to crush the unwary, through rain and storm and lightning, to gain this hall.'

'A tiring journey, traveller. And where may it be you have come from?'

This was a sphinx, a Guardian of the Way, and nothing was to be spoken plain, or understood directly. I answered her:

'I go to the end of my dreams, to the Bridge of Sand, to walk across the waters on a floor of gold.'

'To cross that Bridge is indeed the end of dreams. Further it is than most men are willing to go. To make such a journey you must surely have come from such a city as I have never heard of.'

'Truth comes in drifts of smoke and veils herself from prying eyes. Indeed, I come from such a city as you never knew.'

'Then like us, my son, you come from beyond the world, because there is no city of mortal man that we do not visit and roam to seek out our children. Wherever verse is spoken the immortal ones live. After so great a journey you must be hungry. Refresh yourself for the work that you are now to do.'

She dipped a ladle into the cauldron. She poured from it into a rough grey pot that another woman held for her. The third woman took it and passed it to me across the fire. It was a small bowl that my hands could clasp and feel the warmth of the drink. I raised it to my eyes and saw the stars of fat on the surface of the broth. And as I am a rational Roman and leave nothing to Chance or superstition, I poured out a libation to Janus at the Gate of the Hall. Then I drank.

I tasted mutton in the cup, and bacon fat, thyme and sage and the wild garlic, and other things I could not tell. In the bottom of the cup were fragments of meat and mushrooms, and I felt that I must leave nothing but scoop these out with my tongue, no spoon being offered me to clear out the golden cup, and reveal the fine lines of red enamel, the snakes with eyes of rubies. In the world of true men they would have offered me bread and salt. Here in the outer deserts they would not have heard of bread, so they offered what they had of the fruits of the forest and the pasture.

I handed the cup back, massy as it was, holding it with both my hands. The woman took it, and the smoke swirled blue from the fire before my eyes. The mother stood beyond the smoke, and her companions with her. I could not have sworn that they were three or five or seven, each number being here equally appropriate. No telling was needed but that this was a group come together for no earthly purpose: they met only rarely in the story of the world.

The smoke stung my eyes and I wept. As I blinked away my tears, I saw that the mother was not dressed in rags or in black, but in a gown of blue as dark as the midnight and as soft as the clouds. She was not old and shrivelled as I had thought, being deceived by the misty light of the Island: she was young and succulent, as tempting a morsel as I have ever seen in Rome, even in the back rooms of the dealers' booths where they keep the women too beautiful to be sold in open auction for fear they would overthrow the whole system of credit and leave no faithful husband in the whole Senate. If indeed ever there were. And there were nine of them, all equally tempting. I wondered idly if it might not be worth going back to fetch my officers and the centurions and the troop commanders, for they would be tempted and fall and give as good an account of themselves here as any Brit. But there was no one to send for me, and I did not feel it proper to turn back from this threshold, any more than I felt like turning aside to take what was offered me so easily that it was valueless. I knew that I was fated to go forward.

The women were singing, and I did not understand what words they sang, although the music sounded both attractive and immoral, which made it like most of the things in this world I have embraced when offered. But on this occasion I did not take what was held out to me, although I did not know why. I walked forward as I was compelled, past the omen and through the gap in the furrow. As I went, the first woman's voice came to my ear:

'Turn not back, traveller, turn not back nor ever look behind. Go thrice against the sun and against the moon, and then accept what is offered you within, as you have spurned what was offered without.'

Therefore I knew that I had done right. The path led towards the door of the hall, and was set about with a garden of low bushes. Flowers grew on them that opened from the bud as I passed. They spread perfumes about me that took away the scent of the blue smoke of the fire. My eyes no longer wept, and I could see clearly. The flowers were blue or scarlet, and in the centre of each an emerald shone at me. But when I stooped to pick them, I found the stems wrapped about with serpents, and their forked tongues flickered at me to sting.

So I did not pick them but kept to the path. It did not lead to the hall door direct, but forked like the serpents' tongues, to left and to right. I remembered what the woman told me, and I took the right-hand fork, the turning against the sun and against the moon and all the stars and Gods. It was the lucky way to the north which the Illyrians call the way of life. I walked the winding path, and twice I saw the junction of the ways beneath my feet. For I could not look into the sun, nor lift my eyes to gaze straight before me. The jewels in the flowers held me.

The first winding path was paved with slabs of granite, wandering stones shining with flecks of mica, hard and grey and polished with many feet. When I came to the end of the granite, I took off my sandals.

The second winding path was paved with white marble, of Carrara, cut from the cliff and worked to the smoothness of glass. The slabs fitted together so closely that no joint was seen, as if it had been cut from the cliff in one circle. I went as before, north and west and south and east, to feel the sun on all sides of me. When I reached the end of the marble, I took off my toga.

The third winding path went north and west and south and east. Beneath my feet it was made of a thousand thousand eggs of glass, clear as water. Through them I could see into depths of the earth and sea. Below me fish and dragons, chimaeras and whales, sported and lurched, and waited for me. When I reached the end of the glass, I laid aside my cuirass and my greaves and my helmet, and I went forward barefoot in my shirt.

Now the path went on no longer, but as I looked north it forked east and west. If I turned to the right, the lucky way away from the hall, back to the east and the ways of men and all that was familiar, I was safe and by the path of red porphyry. But if I turned to the left, the unlucky way, as I was urged to turn by duty and by reason and by the cup I had drunk, I would follow the path paved with rubies and I would never be safe again.

I lingered a little. On my left shoulder I felt the weight of the bulls in my left hand, that gave me the sign. I turned left, towards the hall.

This was no ordinary hut of planking and wattle. The pillars were of hard and unyielding iron, and the planking was of cast bronze. The wattle was woven of serpents carved from the living adamant. The roof was thatched with bundles of golden wire, and the trees upon it dropped the golden apples of Spain.

The doorway was flanked with smooth pillars of metal, unornamented, sheer. Within the entrance was screened by a wall of iron, to keep out the winds of the east, so that a man entering had to turn to the left or to the right. Among the Britaks, the woman turns to the right, for she carries her child on her left arm and protects it with her body. But the man turns to the left because he carries his shield on his left arm to protect his body as he comes into the house. Which way? I asked myself. Shall I come as a lucky woman or as an unlucky man? I hesitated before the screen, and looked about the dark passageway. In the passage, on either hand, two men sat on the hard ground.

I looked from the one to the other, and my bulls told me nothing. So I hoped for luck, and I turned to the man on my right, and asked him:

'Shall I be let pass?'

As he was a man, so he was a Druid. But he was not the kind of Druid we hear of in the stories, dressed in shining white with a golden sickle, like a senator on session day who has forgotten he keeps a farm only for pleasure. He squatted on the floor in his own filth. He wore a shirt of tanned deerskin, stitched in patterns with little shells making the curved lines of snakes. His face was painted with fine lines of blue as the Brits do when they go to battle or marriage or death. And one eye was blotted out with a solid patch of dye. On his head he wore a cap of leather, tied beneath his chin: from it there sprouted the antlers of a stag, royal antlers of twenty points. Now all was plain.

Whether he moved as a man at other times, whether we had known him as a man, I could not tell. But this one thing I knew for certain: this day he did not represent, he *was* the great God Cernunnos. He squatted there and he looked at me and I felt his power. He rose above me, he swelled in size. I looked down to the secret places of his hams, and up to his holy horns.

I asked again, and now I used his sacred name, that till now I had not been thought worthy to speak:

'Cernunnos, will you let me pass?'

He did not speak at first, only reached far down and touched my hand with his hoof. He waited while one might count twenty, and then spoke, not to me, but to Those Beyond, the Gods above the Gods. He said:

> *'This man is evil, no good bringing,*
> *Coming through mountains, over rock faces,*
> *Sheltering not from the rain of the winter,*
> *Yielding not to the heat of the summer.*
> *Running from battle, yet advancing.'*

'You do not forbid, then, but let me pass to my Doom?' I challenged him.

> *'There is no forbidding, there is no denying,*
> *There is no permitting, there is only warning.*
> *There is only raising of prayer to the mountain,*
> *Nothing but hearing the song of the eagles,*
> *Nothing but facing the fury of waters.'*

'And if I pass, what then?'

> *'There will be blackness, there will be silence,*
> *Night over Aquin, night over Menai,*
> *Souls that are homeless, not paying the ferry,*
> *Scorpions and crabs fed, decay only thriving.'*

'All that,' I told him, 'I hear every night from my Illyrians. Death's their only joke.'

I turned from him as he dwindled to man size, to dwarf size, to mouse size. I looked the other way, and I saw this one, too, rise in majesty, towering over all, high as the clouds. This was no timid deer. This one was wrapped in the hide of a bull, not long slaughtered, stiff with dried blood and fat. The scalp of the bull sat upon his head, but the horns were torn away. His face beneath the hide was roughly splashed with blue, crude blotches, not tracery. He stank, but not as Cernunnos stank, of power and potency and the maleness of the world. In his stench I knew reality, the smell of decay and corruption, of stale sweat and worn-out sandals, of rank fat and rancid butter and sterility, what is actual in life not merely what is desired.

He reached out his cloven hoof to touch my hand. At the touch I knew him through and through. I was one with him, though we were two. I knew his holy name, the one scarcely used, never lightly spoken. I spoke it.

'Hey, Taranis, Thunder Maker, Earth Shaker, Sea Bull, that levels land and bellows battle and bloodshed over all, that blessed me in the wood. I hail thee, Taranis, I hail thee! Shall I pass thee, God of Aquin? Wilt thou open the gate and clear the Bridge? But what do you here? Have you been driven from your ancient home? Walk you no more in Crete? Run you no more in the streets of Gades? Bull Walker, Bull Roarer, shall I pass or no?'

He pondered, but not as long as had Cernunnos. He spoke:

'This is a poet, a speaker of verses and satires,
Who brings down kingdoms and cities with squibs and with couplets.
What else is Man's business but this, to work as a Maker
Hammering out sense from the world with wit and with learning.

> *Pass, then, Poet, carry on your burden of sadness,*
> *Knowing that after all making there must come breaking,*
> *Pass to the feast that ends in discord and slaughter,*
> *Pass to the acid of honey, the sweetness of wormwood,*
> *Pass to the chill of the fire, the heat of the snowdrift,*
> *Pass to the filth of the baths, the cleanness of middens.'*

Blessed, I bowed my head to him, touching my temples to the ground. The Great Bull bellowed above me. I was filled with the majesty of the noise. I floated in the air, I flew about his head, I scaled the cliffs of his brow, I wandered among the forest of his sparse hairs. I bathed in the lakes of his sweat, and I hunted the game of his lice through a year and a day. I laughed at the poor stag that had tried to bar my way in the forest and to lead me astray. For the Bull of Aquin had upheld me, the Bull of Gades that I had worshipped in his blood had sustained me, the Thunder Bull of the Island had heard me. And so I passed on.

When I had turned to my left, the way of ill-luck, the way to the south and the Illyrian way of Death, the way of the shielded warrior, I came among a band of women. They were many, that is all I can say, because I could not see them in the darkness of the passage. They were small and light of foot, and they came about me like a cloud of moths. They swirled like flies around my head and arms, and lit me with the glow of their gold wings. One took my standard from my hands, and held it before my eyes, and I laughed because I knew that no harm could reach me while I had the bulls in my sight.

Their hands were soft and gentle. They took me from my tunic, not lifting it over my head but sliding it from around me, letting me pass through it like a speck of dust through the looseness of the weave. I stood there in my loincloth, reaching out my left hand, and my bulls were given back to me. I laid it on my shoulder and went on.

I walked on a floor of shredded gold for straw, on carpets of silk woven with a warp of gold. I walked upon the wealth of all the world. The moths fluttered about me, coming visible into shafts of light and then vanishing against the solid dark. They sang with the voice of all the pleasures of the world. There, in the midst of butterflies, I came face to face with a woman who was flowers, who was all the flowers in essence. I bent my head before the flower that shall give us fruit, where she stood in the colour of peach blossom, in the texture of rose petals, in the scent of violets and lilies. But that news of gardens in Rome, of courtyards in the houses of Pompeii, was all illusion, because she was fashioned of the flowers of the wild, of the oak and the broom and the meadow sweet. And she asked me:

> *'And is it a poet you are, then,*
> *And is it verses you make*
> *Satires to shatter a city,*
> *Lovesongs to make a heart break?*
>
> *Come to our hall as a poet,*
> *Sit with us at our feast,*
> *Share with us beauty and blessing,*
> *But give us the heart from your breast.'*

I answered, knowing without learning it a language to make verses in, a language that pattered like the rainbow and roared like the sea.

> *'Of you, Lady, I claim a heart,*
> *Giving's not a poet's part:*

> *Earth, sea and sky are his to take,*
> *And never payment will he make.'*

This seemed to satisfy her that I had the true poet's greed. She raised her hands that were anemones and cowslips and around my neck she hung a collar, a halfmoon of beaten gold, a finger thick, that covered all my chest. It hung heavy as a breastplate of the legion, as cold as a cuirass against my bare flesh, and I drew in my breath as if I felt death. Perhaps I did. But then, I knew without telling her, that I was like her, a God, by virtue of my poethood and her gift. I looked into her face to embrace her, but I could not, because her face was not the face of a woman but the face of an owl. So I put her aside and went forward into the hall.

The hall was a sight of marvels, as far across as the Pantheon, or farther, and higher in its domed roof. The four spokes of the greater pillars divided it into four quarters. Each of the quarters was divided by lesser pillars into an inner and an outer chamber. In the centre of the hall was the place of feasting by the seat of the fire.

The pillars of the roof were of ivory, the tusks of elephants and of walruses jointed and dovetailed on the sandalwood beneath. They were carved deep with the shapes of the serpents I had seen on the cup, and so often before on the bronze and basketwork and cloth within the Island, and painted on the plaster of the walls. But the ivory beasts spiralled and curled about each other, sinuous and scaly. Each lifted up its seven heads and sniffed for blood. I hesitated to pass them. But the bulls of my standard stretched out their bronze necks and spread wide their nostrils to scent the old enemy. They bellowed greeting and challenge to the writhing ivory.

I knew now that I was safe here, wearing the collar of poethood. I passed safe as a God between the pillars, and heard calmly the sound I had once dreaded. Spears clashed on cooking pots. Between the pillars of the outer circle stood the warriors, each almost as tall and as stout as the pillars. They were naked except for their armour, and the blue paint that sanctified their bodies for battle and for death. Their high pointed helmets carried plumes of feathers or dyed wool. On either side, they spread the horns of bulls or the antlers of stags, fastened on with pitch, or some wore wheels or sunhammers. Some wore wings, but not the wings of eagles black and glistening, nor the white wings of swans, but the grey wings of the barnacle goose that sings to men of approaching death and the attainment of oblivion that we all desire.

The men sheltered behind their seven-foot shields, each seven layered in oxhide on a frame of elm, and covered with beaten copper. Yet I could see through their shields and through their armour to their private parts and the thoughts in their hearts and the emotions in their bellies. These were the men who had come about us by the thousand in the mist on the mountain top. I had persuaded my men that they did not exist. But now I saw them enter my own reality. Had I been mortal I could not have faced them, but now I wore the collar of divinity. Not even the two men who guarded the door through which I must enter the inner circle made me afraid. One was old and grizzled, and his nipples were burnt out by Agricola's brand; the other was younger and I could see the stripes behind his back. Each wore a collar of iron about his neck.

I walked the circle of the first pillars, and the warriors saluted me as if I had been one of them. When I had been in each of the outer chambers of the hall I passed into the inner chambers, the places of the cauldrons. These vessels of bronze were big enough for men to bathe in, worked with skill and adorned with living serpents of bronze that held spears in their mouths and beat upon their pots.

I passed through each of the four inner chambers, through the middle circuit of the hall, between the cauldrons of the Island. Now I came to the last chamber, the ninth, the innermost part of all. In this chamber was a hearth of stone slabs. On it burned two fires, one at each end, each in a basin of stone. The further fire was in a square basin, and over this hung a vast and massy cauldron. Little pigs climbed into it of their own accord to be cooked.

The nearer fire was kindled in a round basin. Over it hung the mightiest cauldron of all. The fire burned blue under it and the blue smoke came sweet to my face. In it the water boiled and bubbled.

The moth women fluttered around me again. They loosed the knot of my loincloth and took it from me, so that I stood naked as the warriors, yet not prepared for battle. And they took my bulls and held them on the far side of the cauldron. I wore only my collar. The Lady of the Flowers took my hand and brought me forward to the hearth. My collar was but a symbol of the entry yet to come. I stepped forward barefoot and stepped on to the iron firedogs that held the burning togs, I rose on the flames and lifted to the edge of the cauldron. As I stepped into the boiling waters the Flower Lady took the waters in a golden ladle, and poured them on my head.

Nothing was washed away, but all was gained. The scars and bruises of the journey remained, but the pain departed. I stood balanced on the further rim of the cauldron and then stepped down through the flames. So I passed through fire and water to stand before the place of the feast.

I was still naked. The Lady of the Flowers was by me, and measured my height with a rod of aspen. The moth women came about me to tie my loincloth. The cloak they brought covered me from head to foot: it was not made of fur or of wool, but was fashioned from the skins of swans, with the feathers still in place, soft inside but outside white and shining like the bird itself in life. The moth women lifted my feet, first the right and then the left, and bound on them high boots of soft leather from Spain, calf high, the heels built up, dyed scarlet as the Emperor's.

Then she led me to the feast. Around the hearth for couches were bales of straw, covered with furs and strips of cloth, woven in stripes. Some of the places were filled and some empty, but I did not need telling which was mine. I sat on the right hand of the Master of the Feast, since I came as a guest — sat, as the Brits do, not reclining. The moths served us wine, from the right and not from the left as in a civilized dining-room. My cup was garlanded with primrose and fern and wild garlic.

The Master of the Feast, on my left, ate with his left hand. With his right hand, between himself and me, he held a wheel, that turned slowly without ever travelling on. Thus I knew what a great God he was, for he turns the heavens in their courses, and holds the sun and the moon and all the stars in their places. The Brits do not hold as we do that the earth is steady and stable and the foundation of all that is. Their earth turns against the turning of the outer heavens. This God was black-haired and ruddy, long-moustached, with the glow of red youth in his cheeks: what he did, only strength and youth greater than the strength of the heavens in young spring could do.

He was dressed in a tunic of green, with scarlet trimmings at sleeves and neck. He was girt with a belt of red leather. The man on my right was dressed in a tunic of silver-grey. He too ate with his left hand, for his right hand was of silver, rigid, and gleaming like his hair and his beard. On his little finger was a silver ring and on his silver wrist a silver armlet, both set with amethysts, wisely, for he drank enough to make them worth the wearing. I knew that the silver of his hand and his ornaments was made out of the silver of his heart.

Beyond him I saw a God dressed in black, with neither jewels nor ornament, in tunic and breeches of the same colour. At first I thought that he was Janus, because he was two-faced, looking before and behind, two-mouthed and double of speech. But when I saw him turn his head I knew that this was not Janus, for a door has only two sides, the in and the out, the light and the dark. This one had three faces, three mouths, and looked three different ways. So I learned that the people of this Island have knowledge of magic beyond our imagining. They know what I had not learnt before, that there are ways through a door that are neither in nor out nor in-between; and skies that are neither light nor dark nor in-between; and poems that are neither true nor false nor in-between.

First I wondered that he should come into the feast with no collar of Godhead. But then I saw that his collar was about his neck, but it did not shine because it was black. It was a collar of the twisted heather ropes that hold down the thatch. Now I knew his name: Esus, the Hanged God, that was neither living nor dead, nor in-between.

I looked at the One opposite me. His shape was vague because of the smoke of the fire. But his name I knew. This was Teutates, the War God, with his sword and club. But he was also Death by Water, and though his clothes were wet with water that always ran from them, he did not quench the fire.

These all sat cross-legged, the soles of their feet pressed together. But there was one I could not name, near the other fire, beneath the cauldron of the little pigs. He squatted with his knees high and the soles of his feet turned up to the heaven. He wore rams' horns on his head, gilded and vermilion-tipped, and in one hand he held a feather. In the other he grasped a golden snake, like those on the pillars of ivory, which tore and grasped at the food he carried to his mouth.

So the Gods sat at their feast, and I with them, eating of the thigh of the pig and the liver of the goose, the oatcakes and mushrooms and seaweed. Yet they must have been poor Gods and not used to eating like this every day, because there was not one of them that showed a good round belly such as is the ambition of every civilized man within the Empire. Indeed, even I at my age would have been ashamed to show as slim a waist as any of them. But I drained my cup of the honeyed wine and toasted the Goddess of the Owl's Face, the Flowered one, that sat opposite me across the fire, now in place of the Dead by Water.

For the Gods came and went from the feast, as their worshippers called on them to do their bidding and earn their sacrifices. It was in the wine of my own libation that I toasted her. When I looked to my left, I saw that though the wheel still turned, the God that looked to the state of the heavens had gone about his business, with no word of his going as we have no word of the passing of time till twilight comes — or death.

In that place now sat the Giver of the Feast, the Possessor of All Things, whom we had followed or evaded through the woods and over the mountains, and had brought many of us to our deaths already. She did not eat or drink in her own feast, but sat and looked on what was done, and saw that it was good. She was not tall, but slight and well made. She wore a cloak of many greens, that merged together as if she wore a walking wood. Her ornaments were of silver, not of gold. The bracelets on her arms, a score of them, were of a pound weight apiece. The collar that was about her neck was of silver, and it covered her breasts. The crests that ran from side to side above her head, standing three hands' breadths above her and wide across as a peacock's tail, were of silver. Her hair, neither yellow nor black, but a soft brown, was woven into thick ropes looped over her crown between the silver crests.

I bowed to her, but she took no notice of me. She only sat above her feast and listened to the music the moth girls sang, a music without words or shape or form which followed the winding path of beauty in the wilderness. As they sang, they brought the things of the feast, meat and blood and wine. I suppose that far away, on the Rhine, on the Danube, on the Nile even, exiled Brits offered what they had to give and what meats and fruits they could find. So, it being harvest time, we were served the best food of the earth, grapes and dates and figs and pomegranates, the golden apples of the Spanish coast, and the great moon melons. There were strange meats, whale and elephant, walrus and giraffe, and meats I could not even name. And there was meat — and much of it — that I dare not name. For the Gods accept the meat of oxen and sheep, and they take with delight the flesh of deer and hare: but man-meat they prize above all.

A cup of gold passed from hand to hand. It gleamed from its own nature, not from the reflections of the fire. It was as a small cauldron in shape, but enough for a man to lift in both hands. Each God drank of it, and passed it on. At last it was put into my hands, coming from the Hanged God. I would have drained it, but the cup would never empty. I passed it to the Lady on my left, and she who had neither eaten nor drunk at her own feast drank deep. Then she stood and took my hand, and led me from the feast.

8: THE HILL

Now I knew that I had done right to follow the herons that had flown over us. As we left the fire, the Lady let fall her mantle of green. Under her cloak she shone in an overdress of soft grey, over a tunic of white silk beneath the stiff linen. She let down her braids of hair to hang to her waist, and they were gathered by combs of silver, in a true heron crest below her coronal of silver. I bowed to the Heron Queen, the Mistress of the Feast, that haunts deep pools and quiet places. I greeted the Crane of the Cranes, that dances before the Owls of Athena.

'Ardea, Domina.'

'I am Arianrhod, the Silver Giver. Come, poet, and see what you may be given.'

At the west end of the hall was a staircase, wide enough for seven men to walk abreast. The treads of the stairs were carved and fitted together to show pictures of the Gods we had been feasting with, the Gods we were. Beyond the topmost stair, high above the feast, was a doorway closed off by a curtain woven of silk, holly-green set off by occasional threads of silver, that will shine for ever and not tarnish. The curtains parted themselves and closed behind us. We entered the bower, the sun room that a queen among the Brits has at the end of her hall, where none but she and her ladies may go without invitation.

In the bower, we stood face-to-face. Then she turned me to the west. There were windows here in the planking of the walls: a great wonder, they were filled with glass in panes of three palms square and clear to see through. I could even make out the shape of the great rounded hill of the Paunch. Whether the Lady spoke to me in Latin or in her own language I cannot now tell. In what language do the Gods converse among themselves, of speak to mortal men? All I knew was that I could understand what she said.

> *'From here, I watch the world beneath.*
> *Men struggle up, with muck or little skill.*
> *In daylight, some are blind and some see clear —*
> *How many deer graze upon the hill?'*

This was a riddle plain, and I had to guess the answer. We were in a land of plenty, so I said:

> *'More, indeed, than the sand on the seashore.'*

'Barren, and dangerous, a shore with so little sand. Take and eat?

She held out to me a silver tray. On it were five hazel nuts. I ate them, one by one. I drank again, as she served me, from the cup of honeyed wine, and saw that there were no deer upon the hill, nor any other living thing. The Lady took my arm, and turned me towards the window. The frames opened like the leaves of a door or the shells of a clam. Below my feet, I saw a bridge arching up in mist and cloud.

'Walk with me, then,' she said, 'to the marriage of the Heron Queen.'

I hesitated, because I am a solid man, though not fashionably well fleshed, and nothing like as thin and poverty-stricken as a British God. The arch stretched from the window to the very top of the hill. Below was a chasm down to the tops of the trees. Cloud is not as solid as sand.

'Are you afraid?' she asked me. It is a point of honour (if you know what honour is) among primitive people like Brits and cavalrymen and patricians not to show fear even when disaster is certain; which lack of realism has lost us more battles than I care to name. So I followed the custom of the country and pretended that I was unafraid. I reasoned that a Bridge was but an entrance; so hoping that if the Heron Queen could fly she'd not abandon me, I commended myself not only to Janus but also to Esus who might hold out his heather rope for me. But the Lady held out to me her own staff, of hazel with a holly twig grafted into the tip. Holding this, I followed her. The cloud beneath my feet felt no more mushy than melting snow, and we climbed the violet road upon the bow.

I panted a little, conscious both of what I had eaten and drunk and also of what lay beneath us, but in a short while, as the arch melted to nothing behind us, we stood upon the bare rock of the Paunch, the hill of the Cest. The hilltop was bare of soil. The Lady went to the very centre of the curved summit, and struck her staff into the black stone. It sank in three hands' breadths, and took root and spread into a wide tree above us. Thus I knew that this was the navel of the universe.

'See how things thrive,' she told me, *'on the Paunch of the World.'*
A holy place where love like plants grows well.
Come, look to the west, over the billows curled
Tell what you see under the ocean's swell.'

I looked over the water, and told her:

'I see the waves that beat on the shore and the breakers far out that mark the shoals and rocks. Although the sky is blue, I see a bad day for the merchants as the clouds scud in, and if I had ventured any goods on the sea today I would be consulting the brokers to find if I could not lay off some of the risk in a bet.'

> *'You cannot speak, if you cannot see.*
> *Who cannot speak, let him silent be.'*

Her voice had a touch of petulance, but then she despaired at the prospect of not hearing my voice again, and bade me look at her. I turned my back on the sea and on the wind that whistled about us. I saw that in her palm she held dust, a heap of grey grains as if it were the seed of some plant or fern. I saw the flash of her purple-painted fingers and the dust flying fast against the wind. And then it stung my eyes, and I blinked and wept tears as often before that day, and could see nothing at all.

She turned me to the sea again. I saw the yellow sands, and I could see every grain distinct and clear enough to count. I could still see the blue sky and the white breakers and the clouds like frightened sheep running past. But now the blue water was as transparent as the glass in the bower window. The surface of the water was not the end.

Below the waters I saw a vast and fertile land. As far as the eye could see the fields stretched yellow for the harvest. Between the fields were roads, straight and wide and gently sloped, so that the oxen should not labour on them as they went with the grain waggons to market. I could count the waggoners and the oxen and the gleaners in the fields. All the roads led to a city that was a perfect round. It had seven circuits of walls and ditches. The walls were high as the Capitol, and as smooth as glass. The gates were topped with towers tiled with gold. Within the walls, the fires of the bakehouses burnt beneath the water, and the blacksmiths and the goldsmiths beat out their metals. The men went in and out of the temples that stood at the junctions of the streets, and cast incense on the braziers and fat upon the altars.

This was a city greater than Rome. It was as I have heard of Alexandria and Damascus, which are richer than all. It is on the riches of these cities that Rome lives, because she has no wealth of her own, neither mines of silver nor fields of wheat. She only makes men and sends them out. But this city was busy and clean and perfect, all that Rome ought to be. *Rome would be like this*, I thought, w*hen I was Prefect of the City or whatever permanent office Agricola would give me.* The Lady said:

> *'There is the realm of the King of the Deeps below,*
> *Rich as the silkmakers' kingdom in the east.*
> *Under the waters barley and gold wheat grow,*
> *And the farmers forget their swords when they sit at the feast.*
>
> *Take your men and your horses, Roman, and ride,*
> *Into the deep land of corn, gold, wine, slaves.*
> *Make yourselves rich, take plunder on every side*
> *Where the gold sand opens a gateway into the waves.'*

Only that one word stopped me from saying 'yes', from calling up my three hundred men and odd to charge headlong into the sea. It was the word 'gateway'. For a moment it brought before my eyes the forms of the God that only Romans know, the twin-faced God of Truth and Lies and of nothing in-between. I prayed fleetingly to that God as I remembered him, and I must believe that he remembered me and helped me. I found the strength to say:

> *'That's not our way, Lady, looting for private pleasure.*
> *They aren't my men, except in a manner of speaking.*
> *We're all Agricola's men, and then only because he's given*
> *Command of Caesar's Army here. And Caesar's Army —*
> *That's an exaggeration too. For what is Caesar,*
> *But a servant of the People and the Senate. Not that he takes notice*
> *Of what they say, but it's good theory, and after all,*
> *What is morality but a theoretical statement*
> *Of what we strive for as far as the fates allow us?*
> *Out here in the jungle, and in the Army, things are simple.*
> *We can come near to goodness. Nothing is left to us*
> *For pleasure, but the virtues — Dignity, Seriousness,*
> *Single-mindedness and above all Obedience,*
> *To the law and all that is written in black and white,*
> *Open and shut, clear to understand. We won't turn aside,*
> *From our orders simply for pleasure and wealth.*
> *We Romans, Lady, do nothing of our free will.'*

I had seen beneath the waves. Unbidden, I turned from her and looked to the north-east. I saw the high mountains raise their horns into the sky, goring the rainclouds. I could see beyond the mountains what she had not wished me to see, the narrow strait with cliffs on either side. But the strait was empty, without water, except for a few pools. The sands stretched yellow as ripe wheat from one shore to the other. That was the way to Ireland, and that way we would march. I laughed at the Lady, which was not the answer she was hoping for. So she began to wheedle, and against the faint chatter of the birds in the tree, she asked:

> *'Juvenal, why not be a king,*
> *If you're too proud to plunder.*
> *Take the crown the Gods cast down,*
> *When Cock Wren went under.'*

But now I began to see dimly that I was in danger, because my arms were entangled in the webs of spiders which hung from the branches of the holly and the hazel. I knew that if only I avoided emotion and clung to the clear logic of verse and the cold mind of the poet, now I was crowned and seated as one, could I be saved. I laughed and told her:

> *'What's it like, then, being a king*
> *Among barbarians? Live in a wicker hut, mud-smeared.*
> *Wear a crown, indeed, but not gold — that comes expensive.*
> *So does solid silver, but a halo of tinsel's enough.*
> *And if it's too big and flimsy for your head,*
> *Then wear it round your neck, it looks well still.*
> *You have a judge, a memory man, to recite precedents:*
> *And an augur, roasting the bones, precedents for the future.*
> *Nobles grumbling that you've violated their precious rights*
> *And a Queen snapping your head off every time*
> *She finds you in a strange bed: but fail just once*
> *To satisfy the maids of honour and it's the hemlock for you.*
> *Far better to have a tithe of the land inside the Empire:*
> *Nobody to hamper you, except perhaps the lawyers*
> *And all they want is money to square the judges.*
> *Marry if you feel you must beget your own heirs:*
> *Better adopt: buy slaves for pleasure, sex immaterial,*
> *And if they fail to pleasure you, whips first and then the auction.*
> *True, if Caesar gets jealous, he can be very demanding:*
> *But the same thing happens to kings: opening your veins*

> *In a hot bath is easier than dying in battle,*
> *And more dignified. Lady, you can keep your kingdom.'*

She taunted me:

> *'Baseborn, have you no pride,*
> *Do you not wish to rise,*
> *To stand as a king above men,*
> *A God in your subjects' eyes?*
> *Will you be ever content,*
> *Lord of a little town,*
> *Taking what bribes are sent,*
> *Cheating crones over rent,*
> *When you might have had a crown?'*

I would not rise to that. I had been called baseborn too often. I boasted instead:

> *'That's what I hope to rise to. But your prophecy*
> *Tells me I won't sink to it. It's your doing:*
> *Agricola shall be Caesar, when we have taken,*
> *The Bridge of Sand. I shall be Caesar's friend.*
> *Bringing the Ox from Aquin, binding men with words,*
> *I shall build bridges of law over Tiber and Nile*
> *And kings shall come to me, begging —'*

She interrupted:

> *'The prophecy was not for you.*
> *Nor poet nor farmer shall find*
> *The Bridge that shines in the mind,*
> *Where the gold goes under the blue.*

> *Not for a thousand years,*
> *From Aquin the Ox ill-shod,*
> *Shall build bridges from men to God,*
> *Hammered from words and from tears.*
>
> *There is neither wheat nor gold,*
> *Over the bitter sea.*
> *Turn from the waters! Flee,*
> *Juvenal, if you'd grow old.'*

'But that is *your* prophecy! The whole island knows it, in some form or other. Agricola knows it. Surely, that's why he sent me, with my bulls.' And it seemed a dreadful thing now that my standard was not in my sight, but still in the hall. 'Is this not the prophecy you gave me in the woods? Do the Gods tell lies? Do the Gods not know truth? Are the Gods so limited in wisdom and in passion?'

She replied:

> *'In the wood of the Seven Trees,*
> *We guard what we do not know,*
> *We tell what we do not see clear*
> *But we hold the faith fast till we go*
> *To sit with the Bull and the Deer*
> *And wait till God's death brings release.*
> *To bring your Agricola down*
> *I told him what cannot be told,*
> *I offered him wheat and ripe gold*
> *To behead him with thoughts of a crown.'*

I felt betrayed. I asked her in anger:

> *'Why tell me now? Is this then your last fling*
> *To turn me back from the Bridge? What can I believe*
> *When you change your song from moment to moment,*
> *To suit your purpose. Who are you beheading?*
> *Failing to trap the Master, is the Man better prey than nothing?*
> *Why not destroy me now? Why not cast me from the Bridge?'*

> *'See the face that he sent.*
> *Unknowing, he led out a God,*
> *Knowing metre and rhyme,*
> *Coming before his time,*
> *Restoring the union made then,*
> *When the Heron Queen married King Wren.*
> *Seeking the prize, he came*
> *Cloaked in the Bridge Builder's name*
> *But we know the pathways he trod,*
> *By what barren deserts he went.'*

> *'So the prophecy is vain,'* I agreed. *'What of that?*
> *The Bridge is real enough, you have fought to hold it,*
> *And sent against me wind and lightning and mist.*
> *Fire and water you brought, the air grew thick*
> *And the solid earth melted from under our feet.*
> *Would you have done all this for nothing? I know*
> *There is something you're hiding, keeping from me,*
> *And none of your froth about prophecies will hold me here.'*

Her voice was like no voice I had ever heard, and the verses were strange and unearthly in their scansion. Now I knew what was the music of the spheres, far beyond the song of the sirens. The wind was blowing straight from Ireland, across the Western Sea, and it was full of absurd tales in my ears: of kings and queens and poets and crowns and thrones and inheritances; of warriors with magic shields to withstand every stroke, of births and wooings and elopements and voyages; of paradoxes and contrasts and the pairing of like with unlike.

The wind was cold on the mountain top. The Irish wind chilled me through the swans' down. The Lady stood before me her grove of trees, before the cherry in her blossom and the privet in her yellow leaves, the mulberry in her fruit and the holly in her red berries, the chestnut in her candles and the pear in her yellow globes; and over all the mistletoe in green leaf and white berry, the herb of power. In that strange voice, the Lady said:

> '*I bring you, Juvenal, not the High Crown alone.*
> *But in divine hands*
> *Bliss greater than Roman has known,*
> *In sweetness the West Wind has blown,*
> *That wafts where the Wild Goose has flown,*
> *For over the golden lands,*
> *The Thronebearer's bed is the Throne.*'

And as I heard her, so I saw her. The breezes played about her, and her garments slipped from her, like snow. Her overgown of wings melted, and the undergown of silken down faded, and the cincture that bound her breasts passed from her into nothing. I looked on the ivory and the rose that shone on the trees till it seemed that all the Island must be blind for sheer beauty. And her kirtle faded like ink under the sun, paling the black to grey and the grey to glass and the clear glaze to nothing. And after that her petticoats one by one, the green and the gold, the purple and the white. Last of all the scarlet girdle was unknotted and the Goddess, long heard of, long sought, long shunned, stood before me and offered what all men desire, and what all men fear — herself. Therefore as she stood before me — clad only in that collar of divinity that I also wore, in her armlets of silver set with garnets and rubies, in her rings of silver set with sapphires, in the great heron crest of silver and diamonds set athwart her braided hair — as she stood I knew that she was mine to take and all the Island with her.

But then, so bitten deep into my mind was it, I thought of how the last expedition to the Bridge of Sand was abandoned because some fool in the east of the Island had accepted just such an offer, a crown that went with a bed. And of course, being a Roman, he could not think of union with a native woman, so left her when he took the crown — on Caesar's behalf, he claimed later. And that brought war all across the Island when we thought the south-east quarter at least was nicely settled down. I saw what she was at, and set the Island Spirit at its true worth, which was little enough in the eyes of Janus:

> 'But the Heron Queen married King Wren. What does it mean?
> You that have tempted me north to the end of my strength,
> Knowing I saw King Wren dead with the earth in his eyes,
> Are you not seeking revenge? Will you not betray me?
> Would you serve this new Wren like the last, trussed and plucked,
> To delight the Hanged Man and Death by Water at your feast?
> You can't catch this old bird with such lime. I am a Roman!
> My protector is the thundering bull that sits in the gate
> And where I am bidden go, I go, and I stay for nobody.'

The Goddess loomed up over me, and her moth girls fluttered around her. She raised her arms in the curse sign and I waited as a Roman for death, for destruction, for sacrifice. I stood to receive her wrath because I was a Roman and there was no gate where I could seek shelter from the hosts of wrens that cried 'Tick-tick, tick-tick' for vengeance. But her words were quiet and piercing to the bone of my heart:

*'Juvenal, for that refusal you must fear me
What I have given, I cannot take again.
You have seen me clear — now you must hear me:
Until you die you must see all things plain.*

*Sight is a greater curse than blindness.
You'll see the prize that you can never reach.
Say what you wish unharmed, in spite or kindness:
Living, your life ends on a golden beach.*

*My Godhead's sign for ever binds your hand.
You shared our feast, Olympus is your right.
Gods never die — not your wish, my command
Shall make you live when Caesar drowns in night.*

*Yet still you can be free, and when I call
Come to my castle; all mortal beings long
For death and swift oblivion: when you fall
Arianrhod's web is ready: in that hall,
Ambition's torment can be drowned in song.'*

I did not understand her words. I understand them now. But even then I realized that they were a judgement on me, a judgement that I must avoid, must appeal against. I stepped towards her, my arms outstretched as a suppliant. But she, Arianrhod, Silver Giver, Heron Queen, Spider Lady, the Mistress of the Kingdom of the Wren, receded before me. Her garments assumed shape about her, veiling her as she went. As I came to her, so she passed from me out of the wood of the Seven Trees, out on to the Bridge of Cloud that arched from the Paunch of the World to its dark and secret heart where the poor Gods feast for ever on the leavings from mortals' plenty. But the Bridge grew soft beneath my feet like melting snow, and the cobwebs spun themselves before my face and over my eyes, binding my eyes. At last, no longer seeing the Goddess, I fell.

9: THE BRIDGE

I came to myself again in the middle of a wood. I was lying on the ground. My clothes were heaped roughly over me, my toga over all. The once white cloth was stained with grease and morsels of food, with moss and charcoal and wood ash and wine. And it stank of peat smoke. Beyond the treetops rose the rounded flank of the Paunch. I saw it as one sees things in a dream, not as I had seen the Goddess, wide awake. And for a while I could not understand the soldiers around me. Then I realized they were speaking the Latin I was used to.

'Juvenal! Most noble prefect! Are you alive?' It was Achilles. 'How did you get here?'

I shook myself.

'I have a headache. It serves me right, drinking in the middle of the day. Still, one must humour these provincials.'

'We thought you were dead. You were lost — we lost you.'

'Lost?' I looked at the sun. 'I have only been away three hours. What were you thinking to be so terrified?'

'Stroke your cheek,' Achilles told me. 'I saw you shaved before you left the camp. Is that a three hours' stubble?'

I felt the hair on my face, already setting the shape of a beard.

'How long?'

'Three days since we left you here on the edge of the wood.'

I looked about me. It was a wood of sorts, really a narrow spinney, perhaps five trees deep and fifty trees wide. A few mouldering bones littered the ground, rags hung from the branches. I turned my back on it, looked towards the hill. I saw three or four huts, hives of wicker sealed with mud. One rather larger than the rest, had been hung on stout posts. The sides were crumbling, the thatch of the roof was rotting.

'There's nobody living there,' Achilles told me. 'We had a look. Been empty for years.'

I knew better. But secrets are not for the ignorant and low-born. I told him:

'Let's go back to the camp. A pity you didn't bring my horse.'

'Easier said than done, Juvenal,' Achilles objected, very solemn. 'We can't get inside.'

'You mean the Brits — you've lost the camp?'

'Not exactly, most honourable Juvenal. The cavalry — your cavalry, most noble prefect — are inside and they won't let us in and we won't let them out.'

'You've been fighting with the cavalry?'

'It wasn't our fault, most noble and most honourable Juvenal,' protested another legionary — there were about twenty of them, all looking very sorrowful and as if they had spent the night under a bush, which could not have been entirely true since the number of suitable bushes was limited. 'It was the women.'

'Women? You've not seen hair nor hide of a woman since we left the Severn, not a real mortal one.'

'It started just after you left,' Achilles began to explain. 'All the way back to camp there was women, following us like they always do in other parts, fine upstanding men like us being rare in the Island. And they comes straight into the gate, and they brings that apple wine, gallons of it. But not to us, not the first day. They all seems to take a fancy to the cavalry, hanging around them all the time, watching them and talking away to them in their own language, which nobody could understand. But the meaning was plain enough, and there's many as would have gone off in the bushes with them, but I never met anybody as actually made it. Funny women, flitting about for all the world like moths, they were, all exactly alike and just as hard to catch. Well, come sunset, and they aren't there no more, like the horse-flies go once it gets dark and cool. But not before there'd harsh words passed between horsemen that had got women and us real soldiers that hadn't.'

'Quarrels?' I asked.

'Well, not quarrels, exactly — there were no blows struck,' Achilles admitted, 'well, not that day. But the next day, that was yesterday, them women come back again, they was there soon after sun-up. This time they show some sense, and take no notice at all of the cavalry. They seem to have realized what a fine body of men we are in the Twentieth. The horsemen weren't having that. As soon as they saw which way the wind was blowing, they turned nasty. It was then it came to blows, and they came at us mounted so that we couldn't do a thing about it. In less time than it takes to say it, we're outside the gates and there we are now, and the cavalry won't let us in for no argument.'

'What about the officers?'

'Bloody officers!' And Achilles spat with force and some accuracy to miss my toes by half a finger's breadth. 'We never saw no sign of them, not once the trouble started, not even a centurion. They locked themselves in a hut, and won't come out till it's safe.'

'What are the rest of the legionaries doing?'

'Well, getting back in for a start, because all the food's in there. We can't find a thing outside. I took this little lot back to that marsh we crossed, and there's no marsh there now, but a channel of the salt sea. That shows it was magic done to let us across. We'll never get back that way. The lads were talking about building a ballista, and that's when I reckoned it were safer looking for food.'

I could not think what to do. I covered up my confusion by dressing. As I pulled on my tunic, I saw for the first time that I had a ring on my finger — a silver ring, and I had never sunk to that before. But it was set with an emerald. I looked closer and saw it was my own emerald, pear-shaped, that I had offered to the Goddess, but then it was set in a brooch of gold. I looked from it to Achilles, holding my bull standard, and I saw him clear: a broken-down old soldier, never able to hold a promotion for longer than it took to buy a jar of wine with his new pay, that had joined the legion to escape being sold for debt, and perhaps he would have had a better life as a slave. A man who owned nothing but his own body, and wasting that away with senseless living. He was looking now in anger at my bulls.

'There's thieves been here,' he broke out at last. 'Look what's gone, sir.'

The belemnite which he and Trebius had set in silver to mount on my bulls — where was it now? Thunderbolt and silver wire had been removed. I shrugged.

'Who gives, takes. Lead me to the camp.'

We found the legionaries all clustered by the gate, in dreadful order, with no pickets out. They had made a ballista out of saplings they'd cut down with their swords — about one sword between three men, which seemed to show that they'd not been picking a quarrel — and tied together with their leather jerkins hacked into strips. The doctor had taken his promotion on himself, and was carrying stones. As I appeared on the scene, they let off a big one, the size of a man's head, and when it fell, I heard yells and the screams of terrified horses from beyond the rampart.

'That'll keep them off the parapet,' shouted the doctor.

The other legionaries broke off their cheering to gather around me, clamouring:

'You'll see we gets our rights!'

'Juvenal understands us — he's not a flaming patrician.'

'Freedmen for ever! You're one of us!'

I shouted as loud as I could in the tumult:

'Trebius!' He was sitting on the ground, his face grey. I could see him now, a simple man: being a senior sergeant was beyond his capacities when the officers were gone. 'Get these men fell in!'

'They won't listen to me, sir.'

'You're being *idle*! Get up! They're listening to me. If *you've* no authority, use mine.'

Trebius began to go through the ritual shouts, almost apologetically at first. To his surprise and mine, the legionaries fell in, adequately if not smartly, century by century. The ballista party were the last to come, as if they were reluctant to be deprived of their new toy. When they were all under some kind of loose control, I decided it might be worth risking an entry to the camp.

The gateway looked too dangerous. I found a sheep track up the outside of the rampart, and went up that, shouting my name all the way because I did not want a lance up my nostrils when I reached the top. But I got on to the wall walk without opposition, and I meditated that the legionaries could have done it quite as easily if they had thought: but they were trained in siege works, and the drill-book tells us to use a ballista in the first stage.

The legionaries from their ranks yelled encouragement at me, and someone called:

'Be careful, sir, they've killed Shimshon.'

That brought me to a dead halt on the wall, and I shouted back:

'The cavalry — they've killed a man?'

'Aye. Somebody stuck a flaming great spear into him.'

'I swear it,' I answered, loud enough for both sides of the wall to hear. 'Whoever has killed a Roman within the camp shall die.'

Now I could look down into the fort, where all the horsemen were clustering under the cover of the wall below me for fear of another ballista shot. I could not see any officers. Pulena was the senior man in sight, so I bawled at him to get the men mounted and outside, in marching order with all their kit and food for ten days. At this, the Illyrians raised a cheer. With this encouragement, the officers unbarred the door to their hut and came out. They were a bedraggled group, Tarkul and Camnas, the two surviving centurions, and, last of all, Crispinus. It was plain that whether by accident or design they had been locked in with a number of wine jars, but that the drinking had finished some hours ago. When they joined me, showing the effects of this self-inflicted injury, I did not ask for explanations. I told them plain:

'The men mutinied and you hid. It's a pretty tale.'

'We took the legionary officers into our safe keeping,' Camnas began to argue. 'For their own protection because —'

I cut him short.

'Get to your posts. All of you.'

Crispinus was still trying to argue. I looked at him and for the first time, I saw him for what he was. Well born, well brought up even, pretending desperately to riches he hadn't got in the hopes of landing himself the kind of political post I would be able to buy myself. He was willing to debase himself to Agricola for that. What he feared was disgrace: now I could bring on him that disgrace with the story of this mutiny, and he knew it. I turned my back on him and slithered down the slope into the camp, leaving him on the steps. Vinak brought my horse. I handed him my toga in silence. He would have a long hard night cleaning it.

I gave more orders. Nobody seemed to be doing any thinking but me. They quailed before my savagery as I told them, officers and soldiers alike, how I saw them, with no veil of friendship or charity. Was this the gift of Arianrhod, Silver Giver of the Silver Ring? The cavalry were all out of the fort. I had Trebius send ten men from each century to bring out the kit and arms and food for the rest. Tarkul told me:

'There's twenty men not fit to travel.'

I answered, 'They'll have to stay here. There's plenty of food for them, and none of it on your books, so don't try to take a cut on it.' I had his measure now, the spendthrift dandy, more merchant than soldier, trying desperately to keep one step ahead of the debt collector. A whole mountain of trouble hung over his head ready to collapse on him at the slightest slip, the least unsteadiness in his sleight of hand. 'I'll send someone back for them when we reach the Army.'

I suppose somebody did go back for them. I never heard. Now there was more to do. I rode to the space between the lines. The legionaries were all tense and clutching their swords, the cavalry not yet mounted but with spears at the ready and an eye for a way out. I spoke to them all:

'While I am commander, there will be no fighting between soldiers. You all know the penalty for shedding blood within the camp. The guilty one —'

There was a shout from the cavalry:

'No! No! He shall not die!'

'I have sworn,' I told them.

The infantry roared: 'Kill him! Kill him!'

'Why should he die?' Pulena demanded. 'Shimshon killed Cupesar.'

I had not known that an Illyrian had been killed. It made no difference. I had sworn.

'That was no reason for him to take the law into his own hands. I am your commander. I administer the law, to all. I do not make it. The law is plain — for shedding blood within the camp a man must die. This man must die. Who is he?'

There was silence. I looked at the still ranks. Neither horseman nor legionary moved. I asked again:

'Who is this man?'

Camnas began to speak.

'Most noble Juvenal, you ought to know —'

I cut him short. Arianrhod's gift, her curse, told me what he was. The decaying hero playing the tough old professional before his time, the man who by one act of bravery ten years before had won promotion twenty years too young; he had no hope of getting further. He had ended his career by the supreme military virtue: now there was nothing to do but mischief.

'Let the man step forward. I will have him. Or shall I ask the infantry his name and have them drag him out?'

There was still silence. Then Vinak stepped forward.

'I killed him, Velthre. He came at us with his javelin and ran Cupesar through. I took the spear from him and killed him. The blood was all on the one blade.'

I looked at him in pity. This man had served me for six months, but I knew little of him. Old, now, and too rickety in the joints to ride in the fighting line, never clever enough to rise above a trooper, he had been given this job by Camnas, who pitied him too. Cleaning and cooking was enough to tax his powers, and the other men had jeered at him for it. That was why he had been so eager to avenge Cupesar, that quarrelsome drunken brute we were, truth to tell, glad to be rid of. I could see it all in my mind, the tussling and the pushing, the final thrust more than likely accidental. As all stood back in horror from that first shedding of blood, Shimshon would have dropped the spear. And Vinak, running up to grasp at the respect he had never had before, taking the fallen javelin to stab Shimshon while he still looked at the awful thing he had done.

'Now you must die,' I told him. 'I have sworn it.'

'Juvenal,' he addressed me directly, 'the Gods destroyed you: now they have made you mad.'

He made no other defence.

'Kill him,' I said to the soldiers at large. 'Kill him, quickly.'

No one moved. I said again:

'Kill him!'

Someone from the rear rank of the infantry shouted:

'No, no! Why should he die?'

I rounded on them.

'Because I swore to you that he should die. Will you trick me into being forsworn? *I* will not be disgraced. Kill him!'

There was still no movement. I said, quietly and calmly, in the only way I thought would be of any use:

'Janus help me, a soldier. Do I have to do it myself?'

I began to draw my sword — Vinak kept it sharp — from its sheath — Vinak polished the bronze. But Camnas stepped forward and said to Vinak, in Illyrian:

'Kneel, my son.' It was the address of the augur to the suppliant. Vinak was ten years older than Camnas. He knelt, as in sacrifice, facing the south. Camnas said something low, in the old language they had not taught me. He raised his own sword, struck once at the base of the neck. We waited, all silent, while the doctor and his mates scraped a hole in the earth of the rampart and put poor dead Vinak in, his head between his knees. They covered him. I ordered:

'Form column of march!'

'Which way?' asked Crispinus. He had been silent through all this, as if a real mutiny, a desperate affair with bloodshed and men killed, had taken the stuffing out of him. But he seemed fit to talk again.

'East,' I told him. 'Back to the Army. We can cast round the end of the marsh, and up on to the high ground as far as the Severn. Then I could say no more. There was a tumult of shouting and cat-calling. It only stopped when Crispinus held up his hand. He did not address me; he spoke directly to the troops.

'Others may forget their duty. *We* will march on. We go to the Bridge of Sand.'

With that, he struck his spurs into his horse, and rode off. Everybody followed him, not merely his own infantry but the cavalry too, *my* cavalry. It was the quickest, the slickest mutiny you ever heard of, the fastest *coup d'état* you ever saw. I shouted after the men as they rushed after Crispinus, out of all order, centuries and troops mixed in together.

'Don't go! Don't follow him! We are trapped. They are tempting us into an ambush.'

But nobody took any notice. One or two of the sick came hobbling from the camp, limping and heaving themselves along, ignoring me. I was cast down in two minutes from the dignity of command, from the majesty of a God knowing all hearts, to the absurdity of an abandoned commander shouting pleas after his troops. And what the troops shouted back at me gave the key:

'We're off to the Bridge of Sand to find the women!'

They were going where Agricola had sent us, but that was a minor detail. They were going where the moth women had told them to go, they were taking what the moth women had offered, the promise of wheat and gold, wine and girls. Whatever I said, whatever even Crispinus said, they would go there.

But Crispinus had outmanoeuvered me at the last, he had brought me to abandon, publicly, the march to the Bridge. Now he would go back to Agricola as the man who had done it, the successful commander, who had seized control when I had deserted. I was the one who had disobeyed orders. I had refused the Lady's offer — for nothing. The same offer had been made to the troops and they had accepted it. Crispinus' success was irrelevant, accidental. But it was real.

There was nothing to be done. I followed the troops. They rushed on, trying to pass each other, the cavalry only staying with the infantry because we followed a path so bad that the horses could not make much headway unless led. We cast round the bases of the great mountains, pushing on first a little north of east, and then coming round to the north-west. This path the moth women had described in gestures.

It clouded over as we marched. It began to rain. But we could make headway. The country was as empty as the forests we had passed through before, but the men did not care. Their company lay ahead, they were convinced: each had heard it directly, if wordlessly, from a moth girl.

The men went on as if they were demented or enchanted. The sun sank on our left, but they marched on, eating as they went. They didn't bother about the statutory rest period every three thousand paces. They just followed the standards which never halted. Nobody fell out. The lame just threw away their packs and clutched their comrades by the neck to support them, willy-nilly. The men sang, partly to show their high spirits, partly to keep the party together.

There was no moon, but the path opened in front of us as if we had a guide. For all we knew we were guided — there was no order, no telling who led the column, no knowing if the leader was one of ourselves. We just knew that the men were moving ahead of us, in the dark.

The sun came up, but no man halted. I could not even offer to the standards, unworshipped for the third morning. I could only praise the bulls on my shoulder, as I followed the rabble.

The light crept about us, unhailed, as we came to the top of a low hill. The wind blew the salt into our nostrils. The men peered ahead, and then looked above, cheering. Over us flew the herons, flock after flock, straight to the north. We looked down again, and saw the Bridge of Sand.

A faint gleam of yellow was all we saw. Beyond it, to the north, was grey land, but there was sand in front of us. A wide stretch of sand, as we saw coming to the water's edge, with here and there pools of water. The sand near the edge where the grass stopped was dry, much cut up with the hoofmarks of cattle and strewn with pieces of seaweed and fragments of wood. The column halted. It was as if, now they were at the Bridge, the men were afraid to take the final step and cross it. The troops hesitated, talked among themselves, looked as if they would go, didn't go. They separated out on the beach, the cavalry in one group, the infantry perhaps two hundred paces to the west of them. Crispinus and Camnas were no more now than members of the crowd. All order was at an end, the formations dissolved. Only I stood aloof.

I had come to the end. There was neither harm nor good that I could do. The Bridge was in front of us, and I was ruined — or saved? I had fallen some way behind the men, and I was able to observe them as I rode between the two groups, not halting, on to the wet sand below the line of seaweed and timber. My bulls were lifted high, and before I had taken three steps the other standards were raised and the two companies had stepped down on to the yellow sand. We began to cross.

I rode alone. The sand was wet but firm beneath Whitey's feet. I thought the grey line of the distant shore was a mile away, no more. It would not take us long to go — where? Was there really an Ireland, a land of magic shields and wheat and women?

The guess of a mile seemed far out. When we had come at least that far the blue-grey line was still as far away. But now I could hear somewhere in my mind a sound of land things. It was as if I could hear land birds singing, and the wren among them — the wren above them. I could hear the baying of hunting dogs and the bellowing of bulls and the soft pad of deer hooves on the forest leaves. And beneath it all a whispering, a rustling, that came ever closer. There was a difference in the horse's gait. Whitey was no longer walking on firm sand but in a half-liquid mush; yielding as the violet road on the Bridge of Cloud. I looked back. There were more pools behind us than I remembered coming through, and those I did remember were larger. I watched the pools in the far distance spreading, growing, joining up.

The men were silent now. The talking and the singing died away, as if each of them was straining his ears to listen for the rustle that came in from every side. Everybody was afraid to say to his neighbour what they could both see plainly — there was water all around us.

Most of the land noises ceased. But the wren, King Wren, still sang in triumph over us. The mists were closing round us:

the mainland had disappeared and the shore ahead had vanished. The men were now splashing in the wet sand, their sandals letting the water in and out.

We could see nothing. The cloud was low, almost upon us. Rain was now wetting our faces, blinding us. The water was deeper. As we hurried it came at us in little waves from both sides: it splashed around the ankles of horses and men. The infantry struggled on as fast as they could. It looked as if the cavalry were deliberately holding their frightened horses back so as not to leave the foot, but I knew that we dared not even trot for fear of potholes under the water which might bring us down and leave us helpless in the rising sea.

Then, as suddenly as it had come on the mountain moors, a rider came out of the mists, from right to left. It was a white horse, one of the small native ponies with dogs at its heels. The hounds bayed as if on the hunt, but more like from fear of the cold and bitter waters. As we looked along its path, there loomed up a great grey shape, towers and wails like a castle or a city. It seemed a sure refuge. Some of the men who could see better shouted:

'It's the Goddess,' and they turned to follow her, towards the grey shapes. 'To the castle! It's safe in the castle!'

'No!' I called to them, rising in my saddle, catching their attention again for the sheer strength of my voice. 'There's no safety there. Press on to the further shore! Don't stop on the Bridge or you are lost!'

Some listened to me, and followed, but many turned to the left and headed for the vague greyness, following the white horse which faded into the fading towers.

Now the water was up to the men's knees, and we were finding it difficult to keep our balance. Men fell and struggled to their feet again. They threw away their helmets, their cuirasses, their packs, their swords. They fell down, spat the bitter sea from their mouths, rose again or did not rise. The water came to the horses' bellies. They screamed and kicked as the chill came to them, for the beasts realized what we refused to acknowledge. Still the water rose. It did not come at us in wild waves, but only in little billows, hardly tinged with white.

'Save yourselves!' I shouted. 'Make for the shore as fast as you can. We have been betrayed. Heron and wren have led us to destruction.'

I kicked my heels into Whitey's sides and thrust him towards the shore, careless of obstructions. But the horsemen on my right wheeled half left. They pushed their way towards the infantry, carrying me with them. They reached the legionaries with whom the day before they had been at open war. They did what they could. Some of the Illyrians tried to heave foot soldiers up behind their saddles: some achieved nothing this way except to upset themselves into the water, from which they did not rise. Others just lent a hand or a knee to the men in the water. I felt Whitey change his pace as I wrenched him from the ruck and pointed him towards the shore. It was a man clinging to his tail who slowed him down. I recognized Achilles, his lips clenched and his jaw set hard — who else?

But still, as I called *my* men, horse and foot, to make for the shore, Crispinus was shouting loud:

'To the castle! To the castle!' That was the last I heard from him. 'To the castle!'

Now the water was flowing fast around us, driving us this way and that. But it was no longer getting deeper around us. It took me some time to realize that we were on rising ground, coming out of the sea. I called to my men to encourage them. The rain beat into our faces, but we held as best we could towards the shore. We began to rise from the salt wavelets.

Men who had been up to their shoulders found their waists the waterline. The soft sand still grasped at their feet, and the horses' hooves were trapped in the clinging weed. But we thrust and pulled and pushed each other, and came at last to a sloping beach. I did not draw rein till we were on grass.

I flung myself down, retching with effort and fear. Achilles, still wearing his cuirass and sword, sat beside me. For the first time since I'd seen him in the water he opened his mouth and unclenched his jaws. From between his teeth he took his lucky gold piece.

'So Charon has lost it again,' he said. 'If I can swim this one, I can swim Lethe.'

Men pulled themselves from the water; horses reared out of the sea and struggled to the land. I tried to count them. There were so few I gave up so as not to make my despair deeper. No more were coming. From the grey shape that we had taken for a castle, came a screaming and a wailing, thin at that distance over the water. Soon the sea was high over the greyness, the shouts came weaker. Then the grey shape itself was lost, marked only by the slight foam of a breaking swell. The shouting ended.

I found that I could stand again. I was at the very edge of the water. Now it had stopped advancing, as if it had had its fill of us. My men were out there. What I could do, I did. I whirled my own standard, my Janus-headed bulls, three times around my head, with the sun, and cast it out far into the water. I offered it to Janus, for the dead men. I made the sacrifice for the Army that I had lost. Some were in the mountain, some on the hillside, three in the camp by the Paunch. Most were in the water. And in all that loss, we had ourselves shed no blood but Roman blood.

I made them an epitaph.

'You can't expect much for two obols a day:
Just enough to close the eyelids, and no change over
To pay Charon. That is why their spirits
Still roam the salt sands, fighting the bitter waves.
They died raging, perhaps a more suitable attitude
Than a mild regret for past pleasures: at today's prices
What pleasures can you buy for two obols a day?'

10: THE ISLAND

People came to us, where we sat on the shore. They brought us food: wheatcakes and cold beef and flasks of barley beer and the apple wine of the country. We ate and drank. Then we looked on them with new eyes. They were Brits and they had betrayed us. We killed them, every man and woman we could find, on the seashore.

Two days later the Nubians reached us. We had been all the time watching the waters and looking on the sand for bodies. We could see now that the waters came and went every day, as they do on the coasts opposite Gaul. But never had we seen it retire so far or come in at such speed. At the ebb there would be just time to run across the sands.

We found dead men everywhere, and horses. We did not know what to do with them. When Ambaal reached me I did not even rise to greet him. Dead men, I told him, do not rise.

'Don't talk of death,' he told me. 'Rejoice you are still with us.'

'I might as well be dead. What brings you?'

'Agricola sent me to come by the coast to draw off the enemy from you. It seems you drew him off me. How many have you left?'

We had a roll-call. We made it nearly seventy still alive. They were about fifty Illyrians and nearly a score of infantry. All the officers were lost.

The mist had lifted, the rain had stopped. We could see the reef of grey rocks, under the waters at the tide, which the people of the place called Arianrhod's Castle. Ambaal's men waded out there and brought back the bodies they found.

Crispinus, Trebius, Pulena. I knew Tarkul by his rings. There were several bodies that might have been Camnas, but the spider crabs had been at their faces.

'Yet this is strange,' Ambaal told me. 'I had not thought you would go slave-hunting on the way.'

I looked at the woman's body. The eels had been at it under the castle, in the deep pools. This was not Arianrhod. It could not be Arianrhod. She was the right size, there were silver rings upon her fingers, there were bands of silver in her hair. But Arianrhod, the Lady of the Hill, the Silver Giver, the Heron Queen, had been young, would always be young. This woman was old. Her teeth showed her near forty. Her breasts sagged, her belly was stretched with child-bearing. This was not Arianrhod. Arianrhod could not die.

We put her body with the men. The Nubians piled them together, Illyrians and Italians, Latins and Sabines. There were trees along the edge of the sea — oak and ash, birch and willow, beech and elm, and mistletoe over all. The men cut them down and made a pyre. We poured on what oil the Nubians had to hallow the fire. I offered my regiment to Janus.

The Nubians pushed inland. This island was smaller than Sardinia, bigger than Ischia. It was not Ireland. There were little fields of wheat, perhaps enough in a year to feed half a legion, and nothing over to send to Rome. But there were people, and the Nubians rounded them up to brand for the market. The old ones they killed — there's no value in feeding those.

We stayed on the island till Agricola himself came in the early spring. I hadn't thought the old man was tough enough to stand the marches even in his litter. But he came, and half a legion with him to carry that enormous tent. They got it across the straits on a raft at high tide. It was in his tent that he received me, reclining at one of his enormous meals. The Nubians had kept him a woman.

'We were betrayed,' I told him.

'I was betrayed,' he corrected me. 'I trusted you. I depended on you, and you failed me.'

I turned the silver ring on my finger so as to see him better. He was an old man, tired and frightened of Caesar. Had the Emperor got any wind of his intentions? Would anyone else's word stand against Agricola's? He had been taken out of his quiet retirement, his vineyards and his women and sent back to this nightmare Island, where he had once done something worth boasting about. He had boasted too long and too loud and caught Caesar's attention at the wrong time. He had been sent here for one thing only — not to gain the Island but to lose it. He was to make the excuse to get the Army out, and abandon the whole pestilential place to the Brits, to the heron and the wren, to the Silver Hand and Death by Water and the Hanged Man, to the stag and the bull. It was his fate. The Emperor could not take the blame, but Agricola was to be sacrificed.

But Agricola had done the impossible. He had brought the Army into fighting shape again, he had made sweep after sweep into the Island. He had established a peace of sorts from sea to sea. He had brought this expensive, man-devouring, oil-burning, wine-soaking, gold-swallowing land into the Empire. There it will cling for ever like a thirsty leech. And Agricola will always have the credit for conquering it, under the auspices of the Emperor. How could the Senate and the People blame him for disobedience?

But then Agricola had seen something more, the final chance for the prize of prizes. Even an old man has ambitions, and hopes to live to be supreme. He had built his hopes on its wheat, on the Bridge, on a garbled prophecy tossed round the Island, and even around Gaul, in a thousand different forms. It had nothing at all to do with him, or with me. It will not be fulfilled in our time. It became an obsession with him. Now he had me to blame for his disappointment.

'It was the Queen who led us astray,' I defended myself. 'The Heron Queen was the wife of the Wren King. And he was a God —'

'All kings are Gods,' Agricola mused. 'As long as they reign, the Godhead is on them. But once a king is deposed, his virtue goes from him, and he is only a man. That is why we have no kings in Rome. Caesar is not a king. Caesar can be killed. And so can any man.'

That was plain speaking. But I still tried to excuse myself.

'She tempted me, and lost us in the woods. The guides were her men, palmed off on us — and on you. Drusus was her man. They wore her colours. When they failed to lead us astray, she killed them. When we would not turn back, she led us to our deaths. Only the Bull of Thunder spread his lightning over me. But the Heron Queen avenged the Wren King when she could no longer protect her kingdom.'

'Over three hundred men,' Agricola murmured. 'And two standards ... only minor ones, of course, but still, they were lost. They will never be laid up in Janus' temple. A standard bearer who loses the jewel entrusted to him, and still lives, had better die. I trusted two such jewels to you, Juvenal. Where are they now? What do you deserve?'

'I have only waited till you came to fall upon my sword.'

'That I order you not to do!' he shouted at me. 'We must never admit defeat. To accept punishment willingly is to gain private victory over public interest. Life would be too easy if we could use death to settle any problem, offering up blood to wash away any offence. Listen, Juvenal. Perhaps *you* lost those troops, those standards. But *I* did not. *I* am not responsible. It did not happen to *me*. This was a victory, remember, a victory, that won us a new Island.'

That was how Tacitus wrote about it later. But even he tried to avoid mentioning the Bridge of Sand. First he blamed it on someone else till the old General's heirs objected that the affair was nothing to do with him. So he had to write something nearer the truth, and involve Agricola. He makes it sound a great victory, with the infantry clinging to the horses' tails, the killing of the old men and women on the shore, the burning of the groves. But not even Agricola had the face to claim a Triumph for that.

'So you will live, Juvenal,' he ordered. 'You will go back to Rome, with my despatches. When you get to Rome, stay there. Stay there always. That is the worst I can offer you: that is all I can offer you.'

That's how I came out of the Island. All those years since I have spent in Rome. There were no posts for me. No bribes, no blackmail, no persuasion could open the door for me. But there is only a short time in which a man can start in politics. It isn't many years before you are too old to accept the bottom rung of the ladder, the minor magistracy that will lead to the Senate, the consulship, command of a legion, governorship of a province. It all follows naturally. But I was out of politics. I saw other, lesser men succeed in my place.

It went round that there was something I had done in the Island. Nobody ever knew what. But the meaning was clear. I would never get a post, no case of mine would succeed in the courts.

All this time I have spent in Rome with nothing to do but to watch what goes on there with the clear eyes of the Island.

What goes on in the Island has nothing to do with Rome. The Island has its own fate, that will be fulfilled in the Island's time, not in ours.

I am not now in the Island, nor out of it. I am now one with the Gods of the Island, King Wren and the Heron Queen, the Silver Hand and the Flower Lady, Death by Water and the Hanged Man. Like them, I know the existence that is neither life nor death, neither being nor non-being. I guard what I do not understand, in the realm of the Triple King.

The Island has its own logic which Janus cannot fathom. By it I understand what I see in Rome. Because the logic is different, men here are angry when I lift the corner of the green and silver curtain and show them the reality which is neither true nor untrue. Crispinus would have understood. He is not now in the Island nor out of it. He is the only one I can tell, sitting now at Pluto's feast talking the whole thing over with Tacitus and Agricola. He knows what happened. No historian would tell about it. Only a poet tells the truth. It was a shambles, a disaster.

A NOTE TO THE READER

Dear Reader,

If you have enjoyed the novel enough to leave a review on **Amazon** and **Goodreads**, then we would be truly grateful.

Sapere Books is an exciting new publisher of brilliant fiction and popular history.

To find out more about our latest releases and our monthly bargain books visit our website:
saperebooks.com

Printed in Great Britain
by Amazon